SLAVERY TIME
WHEN I WAS CHILLUN

NEGROES

FOR SALE.

I will sell by Public Auction, on Tuesday of next Court,
being the 29th of November, *Eight Valuable Family Servants*, consisting of one Negro Man, a first-rate field hand,
one No. 1 Boy, 17 years of age, a trusty house servant,
one excellent Cook, one House-Maid, and one Seamstress.
The balance are under 12 years of age.   They are sold
for no fault, but in consequence of my going to reside
North.   Also a quantity of Household and Kitchen Furniture, Stable Lot, &c.   Terms accommodating, and made
known on day of sale.

Jacob August. jr
P. J. TURNBULL, *Auctioneer.*
Warrenton, October 28, 1859.

Printed at the *News* office, Warrenton, North Carolina.

SLAVERY TIME
WHEN I WAS CHILLUN

Belinda Hurmence

illustrated with photographs

G. P. Putnam's Sons • New York

*To Frances Wilkins
and to all our children*

Photograph credits:

Carmack papers, Southern Historical Collection, Wilson Library, University of North Carolina, Chapel Hill: pp.ix, xii, 3, 23, 27, 41, 46, 54, 64, 78, 82, 93
Carolina Watchman: p. 76 (right); courtesy of Mitchell College Library, Statesville, NC
Rudolph Eickemeyer, Jr., *Down South,* New York, R. H. Russell, 1900: pp. ii, vi, 11, 35, 72, 84, 86; courtesy of Rare Books Collection, North Carolina State University, Raleigh
North Carolina Collection, Wilson Library, University of North Carolina, Chapel Hill: p. i
North Carolina State Library: pp. 13, 20, 33, 71, 92
Frederick Law Olmsted, *A Journey Through Texas,* New York, Dix, Edwards, 1857: p. 76 (left); courtesy of Rare Books Collection, North Carolina State University, Raleigh
Penn School Collection, Penn Center, Inc., St. Helena Island, SC: pp. 30, 67, 73
Slave Narratives, Manuscripts Division, Library of Congress: pp. xiv, 6, 18, 61

G. P. Putnam's Sons, a division of The Putnam & Grosset Group, 200 Madison Avenue, New York, NY 10016. G. P. Putnam's Sons, Reg. U.S. Pat. & Tm. Off.
Published simultaneously in Canada. Printed in the United States of America
Designed by Gary Bernal. Text set in Sabon.

Library of Congress Cataloging-in-Publication Data
Slavery time when I was chillun / [edited by] Belinda Hurmence. p. cm.
Includes bibliographical references. Summary: Twelve oral histories of former slaves selected from the more than 2000 interviewed as part of the Slave Narratives of the Library of Congress for the Works Progress Administration in 1936.
1. Child slaves—Southern States—Biography—Juvenile literature.
2. Afro-Americans—Southern States—Interviews—Juvenile literature.
3. Slavery—Southern States—History—19th century—Juvenile literature.
4. Southern States—Biography—Juvenile literature. [1. Slaves. 2. Afro-Americans—Biography. 3. Slavery—Southern States] I. Hurmence, Belinda.
E444.S6 1997 975' .00496073—dc2196-37479 CIP AC
ISBN 0-399-23048-3   10 9 8 7 6 5 4 3 2 1   First Impression

CONTENTS

INTRODUCTION . . . . *vii*

1   JAMES BOLTON *1*

2   FANNIE MOORE *9*

3   TEMPIE HERNDON DURHAM *17*

4   ABRAM SELLS *25*

5   MINGO WHITE *32*

6   GUS SMITH *40*

7   LUCINDA DAVIS *51*

8   SAM MCALLUM *63*

9   CHARLEY MITCHELL *70*

10   FRANKIE GOOLE *75*

11   ELLEN BETTS *80*

12   MAGGIE WESMOLAND *91*

A SELECTED READING LIST
ON VARIOUS ASPECTS OF SLAVERY *97*

INTRODUCTION

In 1936, the Library of Congress, through the Federal Writers' Project, began collecting some oral histories of former U.S. slaves, wherever they might be found. At that time there were many aged African-Americans still living who had clear memories of their years of forced servitude. More than two thousand, from seventeen states, contributed.

Pencil and paper were the writers' tools of trade in 1936; the electronic recording devices we take for granted today would have astounded those hired for the project. Writers of the 1930s simply scribbled out their subjects' words as well as they could and copied them later with a typewriter.

Poets, novelists, journalists, critics, and essayists labored at the assignment. The Library offered a list of questions to ask and urged moderation in the use of dialect. But some of the completed manuscripts lead one to guess that these writers had been employed less for their skills than because the Great Depression had left them jobless.

Workers of all sorts desperately needed jobs in the 1930s. All over the world, governments tried different schemes to get their sluggish economies active again. The folk history of former U.S. slaves, or *Slave Narratives,* as the Library's project came to be called, was only one of many make-work programs carried out by the U.S. government within its Works Progress Administration (WPA). When the Federal Writers' Project ended in 1939, ten thousand pages of typescript had accumulated in the *Slave Narratives* program. The ten thousand pages went into the Library of Congress's Rare Book and Special Collections Division.

Rare and special indeed are the accounts of our nation's citizens who experienced slavery firsthand. Few of the former slaves could read or write: their schooling had been forbidden during slavery, and both federal and state governments had neglected their education after they were freed. So from 1619 when the first black slave arrived in this country until 1936 when the project began, history of black slavery had been written primarily by white historians. Today, thanks to that make-work project of the Library of Congress, the words of the ex-slaves themselves resound in the *Slave Narratives*.

How authentic are those words? Could such aged persons' memories be accurate? As an intimidated minority in the 1930s, mightn't they simply have said what they believed the interviewers expected them to say?

Historians raised these questions almost at once, and the questioning continues today. Some scholars maintain that the narrators dwelt unduly on stereotypes—the brutalizing of slaves, for example. Certainly the *Narratives* give abundant evidence of physical, mental, and sexual abuse. But slavery itself was the ultimate abuse, and one that cannot be dismissed as cliché; and if some tales sound exaggerated, plenty of others convince the reader of direct personal experience.

Simon Stokes, once a slave in Virginia, recalled his days in the tobacco fields. Says Stokes: "Our overseer had hawk eyes for seeing worms on the tobacco. You sure had to get them all, or you'd have to bite in two all the worms that you missed, or get three lashes on your back. That was bad—worse than biting the worms, for you could bite quick, and that was all there was to it; but them lashes last a powerful long time."

The fracturing of slave families might, without argument, be termed a stereotype, since it was so prevalent. Notices of slave auctions, newspaper reports, plantation records, slave owners' journals and wills, bills of sale, and other legal documents give written proof of slave separations that ignored their family ties. This statement of Laura Clark, born into slavery in North Carolina, makes vivid and real her mother's grief at their parting:

"When I was about six or seven years old, Mr. Garrett, from right up yonder in the bend, bought ten of us chillun and sent two white men to fetch us back [to Alabama] in wagons. And he fetched Old Julie Powell and Henry to look after us. Wasn't none

▽ *From its beginning in America, in 1619, slavery focused on serious work. The training of young slaves aimed to get a full day's labor from twelve-year-olds.*

of them ten chillun no kin to me, and he never bought my mammy, so I had to leave her behind.

"Mammy said to Old Julie, 'Take care of my baby child '(that was me) 'and if I never see her no more, raise her for God.' Then she fell off the wagon where us was all setting and rolled over on the ground just a-crying. I didn't have sense enough to know what ailed Mammy, but I knows now. When I heared from her after Surrender, she done dead and buried. Her name was Rachel Powell. My pappy's name I don't know. He been sold to somewheres else when I was too little to recollect."

Amazingly, many a contributor to the *Narratives* speaks fondly of a master or mistress—a sentiment modern readers may find hard to believe:

"I still has love for my old missy, because she loved us and sure was good to us, and it makes me feel kinda good to talk about her and the old times." (Van Moore, Texas)

"We had a master that would fight for us and help us and laugh with us and cry with us. We had a mistress that would nurse us when we was sick, and comfort us when we had to be punished..." (Nicey Pugh, Alabama)

And what is one to make of an ex-slave who declares:

"I think slavery was a mighty good thing for Mother, Father, me, and the other members of the family. I cannot say anything but good for my old marster and missus. For myself and them, I will say again, slavery was a mighty good thing." (Mary Anderson, North Carolina)

The reader needs to keep in mind that these narrators were suffering the hardships the Great Depression brought in the 1930s. If times were bad across the nation, they were extra bad for the ex-slaves. They were all very old by then, many in poor health, still woefully lacking in education and without hope of help.

They might well have remembered with nostalgia their vanished youth and vigor, the simple pleasures that even in bondage they had managed to create for themselves. What good was a freedom that left them hungry, without decent clothing, shelter, or medical care?

Being fairly comfortable and in good health, Robert Falls, of Knoxville, Tennessee, was able to view his bondage in perspective:

"If I had my life to live over, I would die fighting rather than be a slave again. I want no man's yoke on my shoulders no more. But in them days, us didn't know no better. All we knowed was work, and hard work. We was learned to say, 'Yes Sir!' and scrape down and bow, and to do just exactly what we was told to do, make no difference if we wanted to or not. Old Marster and Old Mistress would say, 'Do this!' and we done it. And they say, 'Come here!' and if we didn't come to them, they come to us. And they brought the bunch of switches with them.

"I remember so well, how the roads was full of folks walking and walking along when the Negroes were freed. Didn't know where they was going. Just going to see about something else, somewhere else. Meet a body in the road and they ask, 'Where you going?'

"'Don't know.'

"'What you going to do?'

"'Don't know.'

"And then sometimes we would meet a white man and he would say, 'How you like to come work on my farm?'

"We say, 'I don't know.'

"Then maybe he say, 'If you come work for me on my farm, when the crops is in, I give you five bushels of corn, five gallons of molasses, some ham meat, and all your clothes and victuals while you work for me.'

"All right! That's what I do.

"And then something begins to work, up here—I begins to think and to know things. And I knowed then I could make a living for my own self, and I never had to be a slave no more."

▽   ▽   ▽

A number of considerations affected the selection of narratives for this book—age of the former slave, for one. I looked for stories from those who had been at least ten years old when Freedom came in 1865. A ten-year-old's perceptions are fresh and shrewd, especially when related to direct experience. From a source younger than ten, the stories sound vaguer and are more apt to be tainted by hearsay.

I chose from a dozen states, to show both differences and similarities of slave experience; and for gender, since I wished to present the experience of both male and female slaves. Above

▽ *On small farms, field-hand mothers could look after their own children. Larger places put infants and toddlers in the care of slaves too old for field labor.*

all, I selected for content and for the natural gifts of these storytellers who afford us a glimpse into our inescapable past.

I have occasionally corrected grammar in editing the narratives of *Slavery Time;* I have also eliminated most of the elisions and misspellings meant to convey dialect. Because the narratives are often repetitious and rambling, I have freely cut and reorganized the original material, but always in the interest of readability, never to alter the intent of the narrator.

—*Belinda Hurmence*

▽ *Slaves lived a close life—literally. Families of a dozen or more dwelt in one- or two-room cabins where "you couldn't stir us with a stick!" (George Kye, Oklahoma)*

Chapter 1
JAMES BOLTON

In 1937, the former slave James Bolton was eighty-five years old when a worker for a government project interviewed him in Athens, Georgia. Interviewers were instructed to capture the speech of their subjects as nearly as possible. Bolton called his master "Marse," or "Marster," his mistress "Mistess." His mention of "patterollers" refers to the local patrol of residents and/or slave owners. The patrollers were meant to keep close watch over the area's slaves but frequently used their power to terrorize.

My paw, he was named Whitfield Bolton, and Liza Bolton was my maw. We belonged to Marse Whitfield Bolton and we lived on his plantation in Oglethorpe County near Lexington, not far from the Wilkes County line.

We stayed in a one-room log cabin with a dirt floor. A frame made out of pine poles was fastened to the wall to hold up the mattresses. Our mattresses was made out of cotton bagging stuffed with wheat straw. Our covers was quilts made out of old clothes. Slave women too old to work in the fields made the quilts.

My marster and my mistess, they lived in the big house. It was all painted brown. I heard tell there was more than nine hundred acres in our plantation and lots of folks lived on it. The biggest portion was woods.

Maw, she went up to the big house once a week to get the victuals. They allowanced us a week's rations at a time. It were generally hog meat, corn meal, and sometimes a little flour. Maw, she done our cooking on the coals in the fireplace at our cabin.

We didn't have no gardens of our own around our cabins. My marster had one big garden for our whole plantation. All his slaves had to work in it whensomever he wanted them to. He give them all plenty good garden sass. There was collards and cabbage and turnips and beets and English peas and beans and onions, and there was always some garlic for ailments. They roasted the garlic in the hot ashes and squeezed the juice out of it and made the chillun take it, mostly to cure worms.

One slave woman done all the weaving in a separate room called the loom house. The cloth was dyed with homemade coloring. They used indigo for blue, red oak bark for brown, green husks off of walnuts for black, and sumacs for red. They'd mix these colors to make other colors.

Other women made all the clothes. During the summertime, we just wore shirts and pants made out of plain cotton cloth. I never saw no store-bought clothes till long after Freedom come! We had our own shoemaker—he was a slave named Buck Bolton, and he made all the shoes on our plantation.

We had one overseer at a time, and he always lived at the big house. Marster made us call his overseer "Mister." The overseers weren't quality white folks like our marster and mistess, but we'd have knowed better than to let Marster hear us make such talk.

The overseer woke us up at sunrise—at least they called it sunrise. We would finish our victuals and be in the fields ready for work before we saw any sun! We laid off work at sunset. My marster didn't have no bell. He had them blow bugles to wake up his hands and to call them from the fields. Sometimes the overseer blowed. Mistess learned the cook to count the clock, but none of the rest of us could.

Spring plowing and hoeing times we worked all day Saturdays, but most generally we laid off work at twelve o'clock Saturday; that was dinnertime. After supper, we used to gather 'round and knock tin buckets and pans; we beat them like drums. Some used their fingers and some used sticks to make the drum sounds; and somebody always blowed on quills.

▷ *"One woman knitted all the stockings. . . . I mind she had one finger all twisted and stiff from holding her needles." (Betty Cofer, North Carolina)*

No slave, young or old, was exempt from work:

The former slave Frank Larkin, born in Virginia, says, "Everybody knowed how much he had to do. All the chillun, when they was clearing up new ground, had to pick up brush and pile it up."

Mary Island, of Louisiana, remembers "washing dishes when I was four years old. When I was six, I carried water. When I got to be seven years old, I was cutting sprouts almost like a man, and when I was eight, I could pick one hundred pounds of cotton."

William Mathews, Louisiana: "I was what they called the 'waiting boy.' I sat in that buggy and wait till they come out of where they was. I wasn't allowed to visit 'round with the other slaves. No sir, I had to set there and wait."

Quills was a row of whistles made out of reeds, or sometimes they made them out of bark. Every whistle in the row was a different tone, and you could play any kind of tune you wanted if you had a good row of quills.

Saturday nights we played and danced. Sometimes in the cabins, sometimes in the yards. Sometimes the men and women would carry torches of kindling wood while they danced. It sure was a sight to see! We danced the turkey trot and buzzard lope, and how we did love to dance the Mary Jane. We would get in a ring, and when the music started, we would begin working our feet while we sang.

We would sing and pray Easter Sunday, and on Easter Monday we frolicked and danced all day long! Christmas, we always had plenty of something-to-eat. We runned up to the big house early Christmas morning and holler out, "Morning, Christmas gift!"

Slave children had no money to buy toys or games, so they either made or invented their own:

"Us chillun make marbles out of clay and dry them and play with them. Us always riding old stick horses—tie a rope to the stick and call it a martingale [rein]." (John Price, Louisiana)

"Chillun made the prettiest kinds of playhouses them days. We just marked it off on the ground out back of the smokehouse. We made the walls out of bark sometimes." (Carrie Bradley Logan Bennet, Arkansas)

"Us chillun had a big time playing round the dock. Us played 'Hide the Switch' and 'Goose and Gander' in the daytime. Then at nighttime when the moon was shining big and yellow, us'd play 'Old Molly Bright'—that was what us called the moon. Us'd make up stories about her. That was the best time of all. Sometimes the old folks would join in and tell tales too." (Pet Franks, Mississippi)

Us chillun was always scared to go in the woods after dark. Folks told us Raw-Head-and-Bloody-Bones lived in the woods and get little chillun and eat them up if they got out in the woods after dark. Most of the time we played in the creek what runned through the pasture.

When they had sales of slaves, they let everybody know what time the sale going to be. When the crowd get together, they put the slaves on the block and sell them. They just fetch them out and show them and sell them.

I never knowed Marster to sell but one slave and he just had bought her from the market at New Orleans. She say it lonesome off on the plantation and asked Marster to sell her to folks living in town. After he sold her, every time he get to town, she beg him to buy her back.

There weren't no church for slaves on our plantation. We went to white folks' church and listened to the white preachers. We sat behind a partition. The church was about nine miles from the plantation and we all walked there. Anybody too old and feeble to walk the nine miles just stayed home, because Marster didn't allow his mules used none on Sunday. All along the way, slaves from other plantations would join us. Sometimes before we get to the church house, there'd be forty or fifty coming along the road in a crowd. Preaching generally lasted till about three o'clock. In summertime, we had dinner on the ground at the church. Everybody cooked enough on Saturday and fetched it in baskets.

When the young marsters and mistesses at the big houses got married, they allowed the slaves to gather on the porch and peep through the windows at the wedding. Most generally they would give the young couple a slave or two to take with them to their new home.

▲ *Work assignments generally fit slave capabilities. Musicians and artisans ranked above field hands, and could be rented, or hired out, by their owners.*

When slaves got married, they just laid down the broom on the floor and the couple joined hands and jumped backward over the broomstick. I saw them married that way many a time. If the ones getting married was house servants, sometimes they married on the back porch or in the backyard at the big house, but plantation slaves what was field hands married in their own cabins. The bride and groom just wore plain clothes because they didn't have no more. Sometimes my marster would fetch Mistess down to the slave quarters to see a wedding.

Now and then slaves would run away and go in the woods and dig dens and live in them. The marsters always put the dogs after them and get them back. They used black and brown dogs what weren't used for nothing but to track down Negroes. There weren't no such place as a jail where we was. If a Negro done something disorderly, they just naturally took a lash to him. My marster never allowed no overseer to whip none of his slaves. Marster done all the whipping on our plantation hisself. He never did make no big bruises and he never drawed no blood, but he sure could burn them up with that lash!

We visited 'round each other's cabins at night. We didn't know nothing about no North till long after Freedom come. I did hear tell about the patterollers. Folks said if they caught slaves out at night, they would give them what Paddy give the drum.

I weren't nothing but chillun when Freedom come. One morning Marster blowed the bugle his ownself and called us all up to the big house yard. He told us, "You all just as free as I is. You are free from under the taskmarster, but you ain't free from labor. You got to labor and work hard if you aim to live and eat and have clothes to wear. You can stay here and work for me, or you can go wheresomever you please." I worked on with Marster for forty years after the war!

It was about forty years before many begun to own their own land. They didn't know nothing about tending to money business when the war ended, and it take them a long time to learn how to buy and sell and take care of what they make. Heaps of Negroes ain't never learned nothing about them things yet.

Now that it's all over, I don't find life so good in my old age, as it was in slavery time when I was chillun, down on Marster's plantation. Then I didn't have to worry about where my clothes and my something-to-eat was coming from, or where I was going to sleep. Marster took care of all that. Now I ain't able to work and make a living, and it's sure mighty hard on this old man.

Chapter 2

FANNIE MOORE

This South Carolina woman was eighty-eight years old
when interviewed in Asheville, North Carolina. She
was a girl of sixteen at the close of the Civil War.

Nowadays when I hear folks growling and grumbling about not having this and that, I just think what would they done if they be brought up on the Moore plantation? The Moore plantation belong to Marse Jim Moore, in Moore, South Carolina. The Moores had owned the same plantation and the same Negroes and their chillun for years back. When Marse Jim's pappy die, he leave the whole thing to Marse Jim, if he take care of his mammy. She sure was a rip-jack. She whip me, many time with a cowhide.

Marse Jim own the biggest plantation in the whole country—thousands acres of land, and the old Tyger River a-running right through the middle. On one side of the river stood the big house, a pretty thing all painted white, in a patch of oak trees, where the white folks live. On the other side stood the quarters, just a long row of cabins daubed with dirt.

Everyone in the family lived in one room. In one end was a fireplace. This had to heat the cabin and do the cooking too. We cooked in a big pot hung on a rod over the fire and baked the corn pone in the ashes, or else put it in the skillet and covered the lid with coals.

My pappy, he was a blacksmith. His name was Stephen Moore. He was sold to the Moores, and his mammy too. She was brought over from Africa. She never could speak plain. He shoed all the horses on the plantation. He worked so hard he have no time to go to the field.

My mammy, she work in the field all day and then she have to spin enough thread to make four cuts for the white folks every night. She have to piece quilts too. Sometimes I hold the light for her to see by.

Rich pine was all the light we ever had. My brother was a-holding the pine so's I can help Mammy tack the quilt, and he go to sleep and let it drop. There is a scar on my arm yet where my brother let the pine drip on me.

I never see how my mammy stand such hard work. She stand up for her chillun though. She got more whippings for that than anything else. She troubled in her heart about the way they treated.

The old overseer, he hate my mammy, because she fight him for beating her chillun. Every night she pray for the Lord to get her and her chillun out of the place.

One day she plowing in the cotton field. All suddenlike she let out a big yell. Then she start singing and shouting and a-whooping and hollering. Then it seem she plow all the harder.

When she come home, Marse Jim's mammy say, "What all that going on in the field? You think we sent you out there just to whoop and yell? No siree! We put you out there to work, and you sure better work, else we get the overseer to cowhide your old black back."

My mammy just grin all over her face. "I's saved! The Lord done tell me I's saved! Now I ain't going to grieve no more. No matter how much you beat me and my chillun, the Lord will show me the way. And someday we never be slaves."

Old Granny Moore grab the cowhide and slash Mammy across the back, but Mammy never yell. She just go back to the field a-singing.

My granny, she cook for us chillun while our mammy away in the field. There wasn't much cooking to do. Just make corn pone and bring in the milk. She have big wooden bowl with enough wooden spoons to go around. She put the milk in the bowl and break it [the corn pone] up. Then she put the bowl in the middle of the floor and all the chillun grab a spoon.

▽ *Women field hands worked all day, then cooked, then completed a regular evening "task," such as spinning, carding, or seeding cotton.*

My mammy grieved lots over brother George, with the fever. Granny, she doctored him as best she could. George, he just lie. One day I looked at him, and he had such a peaceful look on his face, I think he asleep. Along in the evening, I tried to wake him, touched him on the face, but he was dead.

Mammy never know till she come at night. Poor Mammy, she kneel by the bed and cry her heart out. Old Uncle Allen, he make pine box for him and carry him to the graveyard over on the hill. My mammy plow and cry as she watch them put George in the ground.

It was a terrible sight to see the speculators come to the plantation. They would go through the fields and buy the slaves they wanted. When the speculator come, all the slaves start a-shaking. No one know who is going.

Then sometimes they take them and sell them on the block. The "breed woman" always bring more money than the rest, even the men. When they put her on the block, they put all her chillun around her to show folks how fast she can have chillun. When she sold, her family never see her again. Marse Jim never

Slaves saw the advantages of education:

"White folks never teach us to read nor write. They was afraid the slaves would write their own pass and go over to a free county. One old Negro did learn enough to write his pass and got away with it and went up north." (Victoria Adams, South Carolina)

"My mother was awful good on head counting, and she learnt me when I was a little fellow. We'd sit by the fire, so you see you might say I got a fireside education." (Edward Bradley, Arkansas)

"When I was freed, Pap tried to learn me evenings to count my fingers. He made me sit by the fireplace and learn to count and learn about money so the white folks couldn't cheat me."(Sarah Waggoner, Missouri)

A Bill to prevent all persons from teaching slaves to read or write, the use of figures excepted. -

Whereas the teaching of slaves to read and write has a tendency to excite dissatisfaction in their minds and to produce insurrection and rebellion to the manifest injury of the citizens of this State: Therefore

Be it enacted by the General Assembly of the State of North Carolina, and it is hereby enacted by the authority of the same, That any free person who shall hereafter teach or attempt to teach any slave within this State to read or write, the use of figures excepted, shall be liable to indictment in any court of record in this State having jurisdiction thereof; and upon conviction shall at the discretion of the court if a white man or woman be fined not less than one hundred dollars nor more than two hundred dollars or imprisoned and if a free person of colour shall be whipped at the discretion of the court not exceeding thirty nine lashes nor less than twenty lashes

Be it further enacted. That if any slave shall

△ *"A bill to prevent all persons from teaching slaves to read or write, the use of figures excepted." Most states enforced harsh Slave Codes.*

sell Pappy or Mammy or any of their chillun.

The Negroes always have to get a pass to go anywhere off the plantation. They get the pass from the massa or the missus. Then when the patterollers come, they had to show the pass to them. If you had no pass, they strip you and beat you.

None of the Negroes had any learning; wasn't never allowed to as much as pick up a piece of paper. My daddy slipped and get a Webster book and learned to read. The white folks afraid to let the chillun learn anything. They afraid they get too smart and be harder to manage.

Never have any church. If you go, you set in the back of the white folks' church. But the Negroes slip off and pray and hold prayer meeting in the woods. Then they turn down a big wash pot and prop it up with a stick to drown out the sound of the singing.

I remember some of the songs we used to sing. One of them went something like this:

Jesus can make you die in bed
He soft as downs in pillow there.
On my breast I'll lean my head
Grieve my life sweetly there.
In this life of heavy load
Let us share the weary traveler
Along the heavenly road.

Back in those time there wasn't no way to put away fruit and things for winter like there is today. In the fall of the year it certainly was a busy time. We peel bushels of apples and peaches to dry. They string up long strings of beans and let them dry and cook them with fatback in the winter.

They put up lots of brandied peaches too. The way they done, they peel the peaches and cut them up. Then they put a layer of peaches in a crock, then a layer of sugar, then another layer of peaches in a crock, then a layer of sugar, then another layer of peaches, until the crock was full. Then they seal the jar by putting a cloth over the top, then a layer of paste, then another cloth, then another layer of paste.

They can most of the other fruit and put it in the same kind of jars that they put the peaches in. They keep their meat about the same way folks do today, except they had to smoke it more since salt was so scarce.

Folks back then never hear tell of all the ailments the folks have now. There was no doctors: Just use roots and bark for teas of all kinds. My goodness but they was bitter. My old granny used to make tea out of dogwood bark and give it to us chillun when we have a cold. We do anything to get out of taking the tea, but 'twarn't no use. Granny just get you by the collar, hold your nose, and you swallow it or get strangled.

The year before the war started, Marse Jim died. He was out in the pasture picking up cow loads, throwing them in the garden, and he just dropped over. I hate to see Marse Jim go, he not such a bad man.

After he die, his boys, Tom and Andrew, take charge of the plantation. They think they run things different from their daddy, but they just get started when the war come. Marse Tom and Marse Andrew both have to go. My pappy, he go along with them to do their cooking. My pappy, he say that some day he run four or five miles with the Yankees behind him before he can stop to do any cooking.

One day the Yankees come awful close. Marse Andrew have the Confederate flag in his hand. He raise it high in the air. Pappy yell for him to put the flag down, because the Yankees was coming closer and was going to capture him anyway. But Marse Andrew just hold the flag up and run behind a tree. The Yankee soldiers take one shot and that was the last of him.

My pappy bring him home. The family put him in alcohol.

One day I went to see him and there he was, a-swimming around in the water. Most of his hair done come off, though. He buried at Nazareth.

My pappy go back to stay with Marse Tom. Marse Tom was just wounded. If he hadn't had a Bible in his pocket, the bullet go clear through his heart. But you all know no bullet ain't going through the Bible. No, you can't shoot through God's word. Pappy, he bring Marse Tom home and take care of him till he well. Marse Tom give Pappy a horse and wagon, because he say he save his life.

Many time the soldiers come through the plantation and they load up their wagons with everything they find—molasses, hams, chickens. Sometimes they give part of it to the Negroes, but the white folks take it away when they get gone.

After the war, Pappy go back to work on the plantation. He sure was happy that he was free. Mammy, she shout for joy and say her prayers was answered. Pappy make his own crop, on the plantation. He made a patch of cotton with a hoe. There was enough in the patch to make a bale. But the money was no good then; I played with many a Confederate dollar.

After the war, the Ku Klux broke out. Oh, they was mean. In their long white robes, they scare the Negroes to death. They have long horns and big eyes and mouth. They never go around much in the day. Just night. They take the poor Negroes away in the woods and beat them and hang them.

The Negroes was afraid to move, much less try to do anything. They never know what to do; they have no learning, have no money. All they can do was stay on the same plantation.

We live on the plantation till the chillun all grown and Mammy and Pappy both die, then we leave. I don't know where any of my people are now.

Chapter 3
TEMPIE HERNDON
DURHAM

This ex-slave, despite her great age, recalled in fond
detail an important day in her life. Tempie Herndon
Durham was interviewed in Durham, North Carolina.
Like many former slaves, she had remained close to
where she lived throughout her years of bondage.

I's been here, I mean I's *been* here. Near about a hundred and
three years done passed over this white head of mine. That
makes me sure enough old. I was thirty-one years old when
Surrender come.

My white folks lived in Chatham County. They was Marse
George and Mis Betsy Herndon. Mis Betsy was a Snipes before
she married Marse George. They had a big plantation and raised
corn, wheat, cotton, and tobacco. I don't know how many field
Negroes Marse George had, but he had a mess of them; and
horses and cows, hogs and sheep.

He raised sheep and sold the wool. They used the wool at the

▲ *Tempie Herndon Durham, at age 103. Loyal to her owners, she and her family nonetheless chose independence after Freedom.*

big house too. The carding and spinning room was full of Negroes. I can hear them spinning wheels now turning 'round and saying hum-m-m-m, hum-m-m-m, and hear the slaves singing while they spin.

After the wool and cotton been carded and spun to thread, Mammy Rachel take the hanks and drop them in the pot of boiling dye. There wasn't nothing she didn't know about dyeing. She knew every kind of root, bark, leaf, and berry that made whatever color she wanted. They had a big shelter where the dye pots set over the coals. Mammy Rachel would fill the pots with water, put in the roots, bark, and stuff, and boil the juice out. Then she strained it and put in salt and vinegar to set the color.

She stir them 'round and lift them up and down with a stick, and when she hang them up on the line in the sun, they was every color of the rainbow. When they dripped dry, they was sent to the weaving room.

Linda Herndon and Milla Edwards was the head weavers. They looked after the weaving of fancy blankets. There was a big weaving room where the blankets was wove, and they wove the cloth for the winter clothes.

Mis Betsy was a good weaver too. She say she love the clacking sound of the loom and the way the shuttles run in and out carrying a long tail of bright-colored thread. Some days she set at the loom all the morning pedaling with her feet, and her hands flitting over the bobbins.

When I growed up, I married Exter Durham. He belonged to Marse Snipes Durham, who had the plantation across the line in Orange County. We was married on the front porch of the big house. That was some wedding.

Exter made me a wedding ring. He made it out of a big red button with his pocket knife. He cut it 'round and polished it so smooth that it looked like a red satin ribbon tied around my finger. I wore it about fifty years, then it got so thin that I lost it one day in the washtub when I was washing clothes.

The table was set out in the yard under the trees, and you ain't never seed the like of eats. Marse George killed a shoat and Mis Betsy had Georgiana, the cook, to bake a big wedding cake all iced up white as snow, with a bride and groom standing in the middle holding hands. All the Negroes come to the feast, and Marse George had a dram for everybody.

I had on a white dress, white shoes, and long white gloves that come to my elbow, and Mis Betsy made me a wedding veil out of a white net window curtain. When she played the wedding march on the piano, me and Exter marched up on the porch to the altar.

That was the prettiest altar I ever seed. Back against the rose vine that was full of red roses, Mis Betsy put tables filled with flowers and white candles. She spread a bed sheet, a sure enough linen sheet, for us to stand on, and there was a white pillow to kneel down on.

▽ *Permission to marry. Slaves had to get their masters' consent in order to live as a couple. State laws denied legal marriage to persons in bondage.*

Uncle Edmond Kirby married us. He was the Negro that preached at the plantation church.

After Uncle Edmond said the last words over me and Exter, Marse George got to have his little fun. He say, "Come on, Exter, you and Tempie got to jump over the broomstick backward. You got to do that to see which one going to be boss of your household."

Everybody stand 'round to watch. Marse George hold the broom about a foot high off the floor. I jumped first, you ought to seed me. I sailed right over that broomstick same as a cricket.

But when Exter jump, he done had a big dram, and his feet was so big and clumsy that they got all tangled up in that broom and he fell headlong. Marse George he laugh and laugh and told Exter he going to be bossed till he scared to speak lessen I told him to speak.

After the wedding, we went down to the cabin. Exter couldn't stay no longer than that night, because he belonged to Marse Snipes Durham and he had to get back home. He left the next day for his plantation, but he come back every Saturday night and stay till Sunday night.

We had eleven chillun. Nine was born before Surrender and two after we was set free. So I had two chillun that wasn't born in bondage.

I was worth a heap to Marse George because I had so many chillun. The more chillun a slave had, the more they was worth. Lucy Carter was the only Negro on the plantation that had more chillun than I had. She had twelve, but her chillun was sickly and mine was muley strong and healthy. They never was sick.

When the war come, Marse George was too old to go, but young Marse Bill went. He went and took my brother Sim along to look after his horse and everything. They didn't neither one get shot, but Mis Betsy was scared near about to death all the time, scared they was going to be brung home shot all to pieces like some of the soldiers was.

We had all the eats we wanted while the war was shooting them guns, because Marse George was home and he kept the Negroes working. We had chickens, geese, meat, peas, flour, meal, potatoes, and things like that all the time; we had enough to divide with the neighbors that didn't have none. Milk and butter too, but we didn't have no sugar and coffee. We used ground parched corn for coffee and cane molasses for sweetening.

The Yankees wasn't so bad. The most they wanted was to eat. They was all the time hungry. The first thing they ask for was something to put in their stomachs. And chicken! I ain't never seed even a preacher eat chicken like them Yankees. I believe to my soul they ain't never seed no chicken till they come down here. And hot biscuit too. I seed a passel of them eat up a whole sack of flour one night for supper. Georgiana sift flour till she look white and dusty as a miller.

Them soldiers didn't turn down no ham neither. That was the onliest thing they took from Marse George. They went in the smokehouse and toted off the hams and shoulders. Marse George say he come off mighty light if that all they want. He got plenty of shoats anyhow.

I was glad when the war stopped, because then me and Exter could be together all the time instead of Saturday and Sunday.

After we was free, we lived right on at Marse George's plantation a long time. We rented the land for a fourth of what we made. We had a horse, a steer, a cow, and two pigs, besides some chickens and four geese. Then after a while we bought a farm. We paid three hundred dollars we done saved.

Mis Betsy went up in the attic and give us a bed and bed tick.

▲ "Our house had one window just big enough to stick your head out of, and one door. This was so you couldn't get out unless somebody seen you." (Doc Daniel Dowdy, Oklahoma)

She give us enough goose feathers to make two pillows, then she give us a table and some chairs. She give us some dishes too.

Marse George give Exter a bushel of seed corn and some seed wheat, then he told him to go down to the barn and get a bag of cottonseed. We got all this, then we hitched up the wagon and throwed in the chillun and moved to our new farm. The chillun was put to work in the field. They growed up in the field because, time they could walk good, they was put to work.

Freedom is all right, but the Negroes was better off before Surrender. They didn't have to think about clothes nor nothing like that; they was wove and made and give to them. If a Negro was sick, Marse and Mistis looked after him, and if he needed store medicine, it was bought and give to him; he didn't have to pay nothing.

And they didn't get in no trouble like they do these days. If a Negro cut up and got sassy in slavery times, his old marse give him a good whipping and he went way back and set down and behaved hisself.

Maybe everybody's marse and mistis wasn't good as Marse George and Mis Betsy, but they was the same as a mammy and pappy to us.

Chapter 4
ABRAM SELLS

The former slave Abram Sells did not know how old
he was when interviewed at Jamestown, Texas. The
field worker on the project estimated his age to be well
along in the eighties.

I was birthed on the Rimes plantation [south of Newton,
Texas]. My mammy's name was Phoebe, and she was birthed
a Rimes Negro and brung to Texas from back in Louisiana. The
year slaves was freed, I was inherited by a man named Sells that
married into the Rimes family, and that's why my name's Sells,
because it changed along with the marriage. Us was just ready
to be shipped back to Louisiana to the new massa's plantation
when the end of the war break up the trip.

They [the slaves] had to work hard all the time on Massa
Rimes's plantation but that don't mean so much, because they have
to work if they was on their own too. The old folks was allowed
Saturday evening off or when they's sick, and us little ones, us not
do much but bring in the wood and kindle the fires and tote water
and help wash clothes and feed the little pigs and chickens.

Us chillun hang around close to the big house and have a old man that went around with us and look after us. That old man was my great-granddaddy. Us sure have to mind him, because if we didn't, us sure have bad luck. He always had the pocket full of things to conjure with. That rabbit foot, he took it out and he worked that on you till you took the creeps and got shaking all over. Then there's a pocket full of fish scales he kind of squeak and rattle in the hand; and right then you promise to do anything.

Another thing he always have in the pocket was a little old dry-up turtle, just a mud turtle about the size of a man's thumb, the whole thing dry-up and dead. He say he could do most anything with that, but he never use it if he ain't have to. A few times I seed him get all tangled up and bothered and he go off by hisself and set down in a quiet place. Take out this very turtle and put it in the palm of the hand and turn it around and around and say something all the time. After a while, he got everything untwisted and he come back with a smile on his face, maybe whistling.

They fed all us chillun in a big trough made out of wood, more a wood tray, dug out of soft timber like magnolia or cypress. They put it under a tree in the shade in summertime and give each child a wood spoon, then mix all the food up in the trough and us goes to eating. Most the food was potlicker, just common old potlicker: turnip greens and the juice, Irish potatoes and the juice, cabbages and peas and beans—anything that make potlicker. All us get around like so many little pigs and dish in with our wood spoon till it all gone.

We had lots of meat at times. Old Granddaddy always catching rabbit in some kind of trap, mostly make out of a hollow log. He set them around in the garden. And possums—us have a good possum dog, sometimes two or three, and every night you

△ *"At one o'clock the babies were taken to the field to be nursed, then they were brought back." (Henry Brown, South Carolina)*

Large plantations frequently designated a "chillun house" for newborns, toddlers, and women in childbirth:

"When I was to the chillun house, we had a granny, and I blowed in a bottle to make the labor quick and easy." (Mattie Curtis, North Carolina)

At children's meals:

"They had long wooden troughs that they poured our bread and milk in and us eat it with a wooden spoon. When they yell, 'Chillun, chillun! Bread!' you bet we just burnt the wind getting there, because us was always hungry." (Jane Holloway, Alabama) heared them dogs barking in the field down by the branch. Sure enough, they got possum treed and us go get him, parboil him, put him in the oven, and bake him plumb tender. Then we stack sweet potatoes around him and pour the juice over the whole thing. Now, there is something good enough for a king.

There was lots of deer and turkey and squirrel in the wild-wood and somebody out hunting nearly every day. Massa Rimes's folks couldn't eat up all this meat before it spoil and the Negroes always got a part of it. Then we killed lots of hogs—talk about eating! Oh, them chitlins, souse meat, and the haslets—that's the liver and the lights all boiled up together. Us fill up on such as that and go to bed and almost dream us is little pigs.

Us didn't pay much attention to clothes. Boys and gals all dressed just alike, one long shirt or dress. They call it a shirt if a boy wear it and call it a dress if the gal wear it. They's all made out of something like duck, all white. That is, they's white when you first put them on, but after a while they got kind of pig colored, kind of gray, but still they's all the same color.

Us all go barefoot in summer, little ones and big ones, but in winter us have homemade shoes. They tan the leather at home and make the shoes at home, always some old Negro that can make shoes, with laces made out of deerskin. The soles was pegged on with wood pegs made out of maple and sharpened down with a shoe knife.

Us had hats made out of pine straw, longleaf pine straw, tied together in little bunches and plaited 'round and 'round till it made a kind of hat. That pine straw was great stuff in them days, and us use it in lots of ways. Covered sweet potatoes with it to keep them from freezing; made hogs' beds out of it and folks' too. Yes sir, us slept on it.

The beds had just one leg. They bored two holes in the wall up in the corner and stuck two poles in them holes and lay planks on, like slats, and piled lots of pine straw on that. Then they spread a homemade blanket or quilt on that. Sometimes four or five slept in there to keep us warm.

The little folks slept as long as they want to in daylight, but the big Negroes had to come out of that bed about four o'clock when the big horn blew. The overseer had one Negro to blow the horn; and when he blow this horn, the rest of the Negroes better appear at the barn about daylight. He [the overseer] might not whip for being late the first time, but better not be late the second time!

Massa Rimes didn't whip them much. If they was bad, he sold them off of the place and let somebody else do the whipping.

Never have no church house or school, but Massa Rimes, he called them in and read the Bible to them. Then he turned the service over to some good old religious Negroes and let them finish with the singing and praying and exhorting. After peace cleared, a school was established and a white man come from the North to teach the colored chillun. Before that, they didn't take no pains to teach the Negroes nothing excepting to work. The white chillun didn't have much school neither.

That was one plantation that run by itself. Massa Rimes had a storehouse where he kept whatnot things—made on the plantation and things the slaves couldn't make for themselves. That wasn't much, because we made us own clothes and shoes and plow, all farm tools. Us even made our own plow line out of cotton. If us run out of cotton, sometime made them out of bear grass. We made buttons for us clothes out of little round pieces of gourds and covered them with cloth.

That wasn't such a big plantation, about a thousand acres

△ In 1862, workers from the North established a school for Negroes on St. Helena Island, South Carolina, as part of an experiment to teach ex-slaves self-sufficiency.

and only about forty Negroes. Us had no real doctor, but of course there was a doctor man at Jasper and one at Newton. A Negro had to be pretty sick before they called a doctor. There's always some old-time Negro that knowed lots of remedies and different kinds of herbs and roots.

My granddaddy, he could stop blood and he could conjure off the fever and rub his fingers over warts and they'd get away. He made oil out of rattlesnake for the rheumatiz. For cramp, he got a kind of bark off of a tree. Some Negroes wore brass rings to keep off the rheumatiz, and punched a hole in a penny or dime and wore that on the ankle to keep off sickness.

Remember the war? Course I does! There was lots of talking about fighting, and rubbing and scrubbing the old shotgun. I remember how some of them march off in their uniforms looking so grand, and how some of them hide out in the wood to keep from looking so grand.

The oldest Negroes was setting around the fire late in the night, stirring the ashes with the poker and raking out the roast potatoes. They's smoking the old corncob pipe and homemade tobacco and whispering low and quiet what they's going to do and where they's going to when Mister Lincoln turn them free.

The more they talked, the more I got scared that the Negroes is going to get set free and wondering what I's going to do if they is. No, I guess I don't want to live back in them times no more, but I sure seed lots of Negroes not having nigh as much to eat, and not doing so well as they did when they was slaves.

Chapter 5
MINGO WHITE

*This former slave, living at Burleson in Franklin
County, Alabama, did not know his age, but he did
remember that he was a big boy when the Civil War
began. The WPA worker who interviewed White
guessed him to be at least ninety.*

I was born in Chester, South Carolina, but I was mostly raised
in Alabama. When I was about four or five years old, I was
loaded in a wagon with a lot more people in it. Where I was
bound, I don't know. Whatever become of my mammy and
pappy I don't know for a long time.

There was a lot of slave speculators in Chester to buy slaves
for some folks in Alabama. I remember that I was took up on a
stand and people come around and felt my arms and legs and
chest and asked me questions. Before we slaves was took to the
trading post, Old Marsa Crawford told us to tell everybody
what asked that us'd never been sick in our life. Us used to tell
all sorts of lies for our marsa.

My pappy and mammy was sold from each other too, the

Know all men by these presents that I Willis Robinson of the County of Perquimons and State of North Carolina have this this day Barg=ained and Sold unto Nathan Winslow of the County and State aforesaid one Negro boy called Isom, he having paid and secured to be paid unto me One Hundred and Sixty Dollars before the enscaling of this. ———

I do agree to warrant and Defend the right title and interest of said boy unto the said Nathan Winslow, against all persons claim: from or under me.— In witness whereof I have hereunto set my hand and seal this the 30th of May 1825. ————

Witness

Willis   his   +   Robinson   {Seal}
      Cross

Wm Mitchell Senr

△ *Bill of sale for "one Negro boy called Isom." The seller, Willis Robinson, signed with "his cross"—an X, the legal mark of anyone unable to write.*

same time as I was sold. I used to wonder if I had any brothers or sisters, as I had always wanted some. A few years later I found out I didn't have none.

I'll never forget the trip from Chester to Burleson. I wouldn't remember so well, I don't guess, excepting I had a big old sheep-dog named Trailer. He followed right in back of the wagon that I was in. Us had to cross a wide stream what I took to be a river. When we started across, I was watching him close so if he gived out, I was going to try to get him. Old Trailer never stopped following. He didn't give out, he didn't even have to swim. He just walked along and lapped the water, like a dog will.

I was just a little thing; took away from my mammy and pappy when I needed them most. The only caring that I knowed about was give to me by a friend of my pappy. His name was John White. My pappy told him to take care of me for him. John was a fiddler, and many a night I woke up to find myself asleep betwixt his legs whilst he was playing for a dance for the white folks.

John took me and kept me in the cabin with him. The cabin didn't have no furniture in it like we has nowadays. The table had two legs, the legs set out to the front whilst the back part was nailed to the wall. Us didn't have no stove. The bed was one-legged. It was made in the corner of the room, with the leg setting out in the middle of the floor. A plank was run betwixt the logs of the cabin and nailed to the post on the front of the bed. Across the foot another plank was run into the logs and nailed to the leg. Then some straw or corn shucks was piled on for a mattress. Us used anything we could get for cover.

I weren't nothing but a child, but I had to work the same as any man. I went to the field and hoed cotton, pulled fodder, and

Many accounts in the Slave Narratives tell of the determined search for missing family members:

"My father was sold away from us in Alabama and we heard he was in Pine Bluff, so Aunt Fanny brought us here. She just had a road full of us. We walked. We was a week on the road." (Ada Moorehead, Arkansas)

"Right after the war, Northern preachers come around with a little book a-marrying slaves. I seed one of them marry my pappy and mammy. After this they tried to find their fourteen chillun what was sold away; they never did find but three of them." (Mattie Curtis, North Carolina)

▷ *Unloading cotton. Growing, harvesting, and processing cotton still required hand labor by slaves long after Eli Whitney invented the cotton gin in 1793.*

picked cotton with the rest of the hands. In the winter I went to the woods with the menfolks to get wood or sap from the trees to make turpentine and tar. We made charcoal to run the blacksmith shop with.

There was a woman on the place, Selina White, what everybody called Mammy. One day Mammy said, "Mingo, your mammy is coming."

I said, "I thought that you was my mammy."

She said, "No, I ain't your mammy; your mammy is way away from here."

I was down at the barn when a wagon come up the lane. I stood around, like a child will. My mammy got out and broke and run to me and throwed her arms around my neck and hug and kiss me.

I just stood there looking at her.

She said, "Son, ain't you glad to see your mammy?"

Mammy Selina call me and told me that I had hurt my mammy's feelings, and that this woman was my mammy.

I went off and studied, and I begin to remember things. I went to Selina and ask her how long it been since I seen my mammy. She told me that I had been away from her since I was just a little child. I went to my mammy and told her that I was sorry for the way I act when I first saw her and for her to forgive me.

She told me how the family had been broke up. She hadn't seen my pappy since he was sold. My mammy never would have seen me if the Lord hadn't have been in the plan.

Back then it was the custom for women to come home whenever their husbands died or quit them. Tom White's daughter married one of Mr. Crawford's sons. They lived in Virginia. Mr. Crawford's son died and that throwed her to have to come home. My mammy had been her maid, so when she got ready to come home she brung my mammy with her.

After my mammy come, I helped her with her work. Her task was too hard for any one person. She had to serve as maid to Mr. White's daughter, cook for all of the hands, spin and card four cuts of thread a day—144 threads to the cut—and then wash. No matter what she had to do the next day, she would have to get them four cuts of thread, even on wash day.

Wash day was on Wednesday. My mammy would take the clothes about three-quarters of a mile to the branch where the washing was to be done. She had a paddle what she beat the clothes with. Everybody could hear the paddle for miles. *Pow-pow-pow,* that's how it sound. She had to iron the clothes the same day that she washed.

It was hard back in them days. Every morning before daybreak you had to be up and ready to get to the field. After the day's work, there weren't anything for the slaves to do but go to bed. We had to be in bed by nine o'clock. Every night the drivers come around to make sure that we was in the bed. It was the same every day in the year except on Sunday. On Christmas we didn't have to do no work; no more than feed the stock and do the little work around the house.

The owners of slaves used to give corn-shucking parties and invite slaves from other plantations. They would have plenty of whiskey and stuff to eat. The slaves would shuck corn and eat and drink. They used to give cotton pickings the same way. All of this went on at night. They had jacklights in the cotton patch for us to see by. The lights was made on a forked stick and moved from place to place whilst we picked. The corn shucking was done at the barn, so they didn't have to have the lights moved from place to place.

The white folks didn't learn us to do nothing but work. They said that us weren't supposed to know how to read and write.

Before the Yankees come, the white folks took all their clothes and hung them in the cabins. They told the colored folks to tell the Yankees the clothes was theirs [belonged to the slaves]. They told us to tell them how good they been to us and that we liked to live with them.

I was a pretty big boy when the war broke out. I remember seeing the Yankees cross Big Bear Creek Bridge one day. All of the soldiers crossed the bridge but one. He stayed on the other side till the rest had got across, then he got down off his horse and took a bottle of something and strowed it all over the bridge. Then he lighted a match to it. In a few minutes the Rebel soldiers come to the bridge, but it was on fire, and they had to swim across to the other side.

I went home and told my mammy that the Rebels was chasing

the Union soldiers and that one of the Unions had poured some water on the bridge and set it afire. She laugh and say, "Son, don't you know water don't make a fire? That must have been turpentine, or oil!"

Old Ned White slipped off and went to join the Union army. After Ned had got to the North, the other hands begin to watch for a chance to slip off. Many a one was caught and brung back. I saw Ned after the war and he told me the night he left, the patterollers runned him for four days. The patterollers used to be bad. They would run the folks if they was caught out after eight o'clock in the night, if they didn't have no pass from the marsa.

One day Mr. Tom was having a big barbecue for the Rebel soldiers in our yard. Come a big roaring down the military road, and three men in blue coats rode up to the gate and on in. Just as soon as the Rebels saw them, they all run to the woods. In about five minutes, the yard was full of blue coats. They ate up all the grub what the Rebels had been eating. Tom White had to run away to keep the Yankees from getting him.

The day we got news that we was free, Mr. White called us to the house. He said, "You are all free, just as free as I am. Now go and get yourself somewhere to stick your heads."

As soon as he say that, my mammy hollered out, "That's enough for a yearling!" She struck out across the field to Mr. Lee Osborn's to get a place for me and her to stay.

He paid us seventy-five cents a day, fifty cents to her, and two bits for me. He gave us our dinner along with the wages. After the crop was gathered for that year, me and my mammy cut and hauled wood for Mr. Osborn.

Us left Mr. Osborn that fall and went to Mr. John Rawlins. Us made a sharecrop with him. Us'd pick two rows of cotton, and he'd pick two rows. Us'd pull two rows of corn, and he'd pull two rows. He furnished us with rations and a place to stay. Us'd sell our cotton and corn and pay Mr. John Rawlins for feeding us.

We moved with Mr. Hugh Nelson and made a sharecrop with him. We kept moving and making sharecrops till us saved up enough money to rent us a place and make a crop for ourselves. Us did right well at this until the Ku Klux got so bad, us had to move back with Mr. Nelson for protection.

The men that took us in was Union men. They lived here in the South, but they took our part in the slave business. The Ku Klux threaten to whip Mr. Nelson because he took up for the Negroes. Heap of nights we would hear of the Ku Klux coming and leave home. Sometimes us was scared to go away from home, and scared not to.

One day I borrowed a gun from Ed Davis to go squirrel hunting. When I taken the gun back, I didn't unload it like I always been doing. That night the Ku Klux called on Ed. He heard one of them say, "Shoot him time he gets the door open."

"Open the door," he heard one of them say.

He says, "Wait till I can light the lamp." Then he got the gun what I had left loaded, stuck it through a log, and pull the trigger. He hit Newt Dobbs in the stomach and killed him. He couldn't stay around Burleson anymore, so he come to Mr. Nelson and got enough money to get to Pine Bluff, Arkansas. The Ku Klux got bad sure enough then, and went to killing Negroes and white folks too.

Slavery wouldn't have been so bad, but folks made it so by selling us for high prices, and of course folks had to try to get their money's worth out of them.

Booker T. Washington did one of the greatest things when he fix it for Negro boys and girls to learn how to get on in the world. Abe Lincoln was as noble a man as ever walked. The chillun of Israel was in bondage one time and God sent Moses to deliver them. Well, I suppose that God sent Abe Lincoln to deliver us.

Chapter 6
GUS SMITH

*Gus Smith would have been ninety or ninety-one
at the time of this interview in Rolla, Missouri.*

I was born on the Fourth of July in 1845, near Rich Fountain, Osage County, Missouri, not far from Jefferson City. My father's name was Jim Messersmith, and my mother's maiden name was Martha Williams. I was called August Messersmith until I was old enough to vote; then I changed it to plain Gus Smith.

My master's name was Bill Messersmith and he called hisself a Pennsylvania Dutchman. His father settled in Missouri, near Jefferson City, many years before the war. He owned fifteen hundred acres of land. The old man, my master's father, had a good many slaves but the chillun didn't have so many after the old man died. My master's brother took one of the Negro boys; his sister took a Negro girl. Zennie, another sister, took a girl and a boy, and my master took my father and mother.

My father and mother had their own cabin to live in with their family. The hewed log house we lived in was very big,

△ *For years, slaves made their clothing "from scratch." The carding comb straight-ened cotton or wool fibers for spinning thread to be used in weaving.*

**Their abrupt liberation in 1865 stunned
and confused many slaves:**

"There is plenty Negroes in Louisiana that is still slaves. A spell back, I made a trip to where I was raised, to see my old missy before she died, and there was Negroes in twelve or fourteen miles of that place that they didn't know they is free. There is plenty Negroes around here [in Texas] what is same as slaves and has worked for white folks twenty and twenty-five years and ain't drawed a five-cent piece, just old clothes and something to eat. That's the way we was in slavery." (Willis Winn, Louisiana) about five or six rooms. We all wore homespun clothes. Mother carded, spun, and wove all our clothes. Mother was the cook at our place.

In busy season we had to be up and ready to work at daybreak. There was plenty of work for everyone then, even to the little darkies, if only to pull weeds. We raised wheat, corn, cotton, tobacco, cabbage, potatoes, sheep, hogs, and cattle. Had plenty of everything to eat.

We had good times along with the work. During Christmastime and the whole month of January, it was the ruling to give the slaves a holiday in our part of the country. A whole month, to go as far as we wanted to, but we had better be back by the first of February. If we wanted to go through a territory where it was hard to travel or get by, we got a pass from our master.

My master let us come and go pretty much as we pleased. In fact, we had much more freedom than most of the slaves had in those days. He let us go to other places to work when we had nothing to do at home, and we kept our money we earned and spent it to suit ourselves. We had it so much better that our neighbors would not let their slaves associate with us, for fear we would put devilment in their heads.

We had quiltings, dancing, and making rails for days at a time. We don't have nothing to eat now like we did then. My goodness! Women in those days could cook. Great big pound cakes a foot and a half high. All kinds of game, wild ducks, geese, squirrels, rabbits, possum, pigeons. I have seen the wild pigeons so thick they looked like storm clouds coming. I remember my father shooting so many that my mother just fed them to the hogs. Ducks and geese the same way.

In times of our holidays, we always had our own musicians. Sometimes we sent ten or twelve miles for a fiddler. He'd stay a week or two in one place and then he would go on to the next farm, maybe four or five miles away, and they had a good time for a week.

White folks and colored folks came to these gatherings from miles around, sat up all night dancing, eating, and drinking. People kept whiskey by the barrel. You see, in those days they just loaded up ten or twelve bushel of corn, took it to the stillhouse, and traded it for a barrel of whiskey. Everything was traded, even to labor. Our folks would tell us to go and help so-and-so; and we done it.

People were sold like cattle or hogs, in time of slavery. Our master would not sell any of us. He did not believe in separating us and tried to keep us together. He didn't have any trouble with his slaves at all. He was as good a man as ever lived.

He married before the war but his first wife died a few months later. He married a year after his wife died. He went to Pennsylvania and came back and went to California for about a year. Before he left, he made my father boss. My father stayed on the place and took care of everything. He was boss all during the war.

When the battle of Wilson Creek was fought up near Springfield, most all the soldiers passed by our house. After they passed, then came the bushwhackers. They stole all the Negroes they could, running them down south to sell. They came to our place in the morning; it must have been about 1862–63. The whole family of colored folks was home, excepting my father.

They looked across the road and seen another house and asked us whose it was. We told them it was our master's house. Our house was about a quarter of a mile from the master's. They saw we had a mare in the yard and told us to saddle her up. And told my oldest brother to be ready to go with them when they come back. They went halfway to my master's house and for some reason wheeled. My mother seen them and said, "Here they come!"

She said to my oldest brother, "Get under that puncheon floor. Maybe they won't take August." (Meaning me.) I was about twelve or thirteen years old then.

We had a great big hearth; the rocks and puncheon came right up to it. My mother raised one end of a puncheon and my brother hid there under the floor. The bushwhackers searched everyplace, even raised the floor and looked under, but my brother had crawled so far up in the corner they did not see him.

They asked my mother where he was and said, "By God, we want to know!"

Mother said she sent him to the field to get some corn for the hogs and told me to run down there and look for him.

Well, I did. I run down in that field and I stayed out in the woods for four days and nights with nothing to eat but what wild grapes and hazelnuts I could find. I knew better than to go back, but I did not know where to go.

I fell on a plan to go to my young missus, Zennie. They lived off the main road, two miles from where we lived. I got to her home in the evening, about four o'clock. I saw my cousin Melie, fifteen or sixteen years old, out a piece from the barn, but was afraid to let her see me. I stayed all night in the barn, and next morning I peeped out and saw her again. She was picking beans.

I hollered and she recognized me, told me to come on out, that my mother and all of them was at their house then. My oldest brother, Jim, was there too.

I went down to the house and they fixed me something to eat, but only a little; they were afraid it might make me sick. My mother told me to stay with Miss Zennie.

Miss Zennie had married the second time to a man by the name of George McGee. Her first husband, Dave Goodman, was killed right at the start of the war by a gang of robbers something like the bushwhackers, who went in gangs of ten and fifteen, stealing Negroes or anything else they could get their hands on.

George McGee and my brother Jim hid out in the bluffs at Rollins' Ferry, a place where ferryboats ran. George McGee hid because he did not want to go in the army. They both came to the house for provisions about twelve o'clock that night and took me with them. We camped out that night, and next morning they said to me, "You stay here. They is out of meat at the house." So they went back to the house and killed and dressed a young heifer and came back at night to get me.

We had a good time, eating supper and playing. Along in the night I heard something like horses' hooves hitting the ground. I told my mother.

She said, "You don't hear nothing."

George McGee, the young master, said, "Wait, he is right. I hear something too!"

We jumped up and went out and down a steep hollow and made it back to our camp. Next night we went back to see how the folks was getting on and found out it was my own father and our own master who had come hunting for us. If we had known, we would not have run.

My master told Miss Zennie to keep us hid out of the way, that we were doing all right. I stayed in that bluff about two years, until the close of the war. I never saw my father and master for over a year. My father had to hide out too. He kept the stock out in the bushes, watching after the master's affairs while he was away. I saw my mother every time I went to the house for something to eat, about twelve o'clock at night.

We stayed hid until they took General Lee. Then we went back to Old Master's house, and it was not long until peace was declared.

One morning, Old Master come over early and said, "Jim, by God! You are a free man this morning, as free as I am. I can't hold you any longer. Now take your family and go over on that one hundred and sixty acres I bought and go to work."

He was giving us all a chance to pay out the farm for ourselves a home. My father said, "There's nothing to go with it to help clear it and live."

Old Master answered, "There's the smokehouse. Take all you want and I'll furnish you with everything else you need for a year, until you get a start. I've got all the land my heart could wish but none of it is cleared off. Go down there with your boys and I'll send two men and you clear off that land. I'll give you five years' lease. All you clear, you can have half."

Well, we cleared fifty acres that winter. There was six of us— my cousin, my father, brother, myself, and the two men. We had

▽ *The yard as laundry.* "Ma put out big washings, on the bushes and on the fences. They had paling fence around the garden." (Carrie Bennet, Arkansas)

it cleared by the first of March, all ready to plow in 1865. We made rails, fenced it, and put it in corn. Father cleared thirty acres on his place the same year and sowed it all. We hoed it by hand. We worked out every little weed. The first year we got 817 bushel of wheat and 1,500 bushel of corn. Corn really growed in them days; it was all new land.

My granddad Godfry owned a place called the old potter's place, near Vichey Springs, not far from where we lived. He bought it from a man who used to make pottery. Grandfather made his own mill to grind grain for bread. In those days, there was no steam-operated mills and few water mills. Sometimes we had to go as much as twenty miles to grind a bushel of corn. So Grandfather made his own burr to grind corn and wheat.

It was as big as any burr in the large mills, but it was turned by hand power. It was made of limestone rock, a great big stone two and a half foot across. The top burr would probably weigh about three or four hundred pounds. The bottom case would weigh a thousand pounds or more.

There was a hole in the top stone, where the grain flowed freely to the bottom and ground out on the big thick stone below. I ground many a bushel of meal on it myself. I don't know how Grandfather got the large stones in place; it was there as long as I could remember. I just wonder if it isn't someplace there yet. I would love to go and find out and see the old burr again.

People call these hard times—shucks, they don't know what hard times is. Those were hard days, when folks had to go twenty miles to mill on foot. I remember in my early days, we used cattle for teams to haul; start at four o'clock in the morning, drive all day, stay overnight, and grind the next day. Sometimes the crowd ahead of us was so big we had to stay over for three or four days. Sometimes we would be until eleven or twelve at night getting home. Gone at least two days and one night. I had to make trips like this many times.

Sometimes we could take a couple of bushel of corn and go on horseback, but twice a year, spring and fall, we would take eight or ten bushel of wheat, six and eight bushel of corn, or according to what we needed, and take the cattle and a old wooden-axle wagon, walking and driving the cattle all the way there and back. We drove or led them with only a rope around them.

The last trip I made milling, I drove for Bill Fannins, a yoke of young three-year-old cattle, wasn't even broke. Went twenty-five miles, drove all the way, walking, while he sat up in the wagon. Sometimes the wagon dragged in the mud, the old wooden axle burying so deep we couldn't hardly get it out, going through timber and dodging brush. Some folks went even farther than that. A mill might be four or five miles from you, but they got out of fix and you would have to go to another one. Maybe twenty-five miles or more.

My grandfather was an old-fashioned herb doctor, one of the best doctors of his kind. Everybody knew him in that country, and he doctored among the white people. He was seldom at home. Lots of cases that other doctors gave up, he went and raised them. He could cure anything.

Grandfather could "blow out" fire. It was a secret charm, handed down from generation to generation. My grandfather simply blew on the burn and the fire and pain was gone. He told my aunt Harriet and she could blow fire the same as my grandfather. Only one could be told.

When I was sick one time, my folks had Dr. Boles from Lane's Prairie and Dr. Mayweather from Vichey to come and tend me. They both gave me up. I had typhoid and pneumonia. These doctors were the best to be found, but they could do nothing and said I was as good as dead.

My grandfather had come to Rolla, doctoring Charley Stroback's child. He got home about four o'clock in the morning after the doctors had done give me up. He felt my pulse—no pulse, but he said I felt warm. He asked my grandmother if she had any light bread baked. He told her to butter it and lay the butter side down over my mouth, and if it melted, I was still living.

Soon she said, "Yes, he is still alive."

"Now get a little whiskey and butter and beat it together good. Drop just two drops in his mouth, and in four hours drop two more."

He sat beside me, laid his hands on my breast. The next day I began to come around.

▽   ▽   ▽

A lot of the old herb remedies my grandfather used, I can still remember. He used one called white root. It is a bush that grows here. In the spring of the year, when its leaves bloom out, in the morning hours when the sun shines on it, it looks just like bright tin. It has an awful bitter taste. It was used for mighty near any ailment.

He had another herb he used, called remedy weed. It is a bright green weed that grows around springs, also used for many ailments. Another one was sarsaparilla root. He used goldenseal, found in places here. Very costly, worth seven dollars to eight dollars a pound now. For sore throat or quinsy, he had some sort of tea.

Dogwood buds, used as a laxative. Ginseng was another remedy. I do not know what it was used for, but it was powerful good. One was called spicewood. It was also a healthful drink, like store tea. You gather it in the fall, using the stem or stocky part, break it up and dry it. I used it all the time while I worked on the river at the tourist camps. It has a fine flavor, and it's good for you.

Indian turnip grows in the woods here, great places of it, looks like turnips, grows in big bunches and bright red. Colored folks used Indian turnip in slave times. They would take this and dry it, pulverize it, and tie it around their feet. No bloodhound could trail a bit farther after smelling it. It was strong like red pepper, burns like everything, and colored folks running away used it all the time.

Grandfather also used butternut root; some call it white walnut. You take one dose of this and it will cure the worst case of chills, no matter how bad. Take two tablespoons for a dose. Oh man, but it is bitter! It is as severe as croton oil. By golly, it clears you out, won't leave a thing in you.

He went to the woods and gathered it all hisself, getting wild cherry bark, dittany, pennyroyal, and chamomile root. He gathered and dried some to make teas and others to put in whiskey. For rheumatism, he used pokeweed root, dried and put in whiskey. There were many more remedies, but I can't recall them now.

My master's father, before he died, told his chillun that at his death he wanted each child to put their slaves out to work until they earned eight hundred dollars apiece. In that way each slave paid it themselves, to earn their own freedom. He did not believe it was right to keep them in slavery all their lives. But the war came, and they were free without having to work it out.

Chapter 7
LUCINDA DAVIS

Lucinda Davis is only one of a number of ex-slaves reporting ownership by Native American masters. Her master, a Creek, lived in eastern Oklahoma's Indian Territory. At the close of the Civil War, the Creeks agreed by treaty with the U.S. government to grant their former slaves full legal membership in their tribe. This treaty may account for the allotment of land which Davis mentions in her story. She was about eighty-nine years old when interviewed in Tulsa, Oklahoma, in the mid-1930s.

I belonged to a full-blood Creek Indian and didn't know nothing but Creek talk long after the Civil War. My mistress was part white and knowed English talk, but she never did talk it because none of the people talked it. I heared it sometime, but it sounded like wild shoats scared at something in the cedar brake.

My mammy's name was Serena, and she belonged to some of the Gouge family. They was big people in the Upper Creek. My pappy was named Stephany. I think he take that name because when he little, his mammy call him "Istifani." That means a skeleton, and he was a skinny man. He belonged to the Grayson family; they big people in the Creek, and with the white folks too.

The way the Creek made the name for young boys, when the boy got old enough, the big men in the town give him a name. Sometime later on they stick on more name. If he a good talker, they stick on "-yoholo," and if he make lots of jokes, they call him "-hadjo." If he is a good leader, they call him "-imala," and if he kind of mean, they sometime call him "fixigo."

My mammy and pappy belonged to two masters, but they lived together on a place. They work patches and give the masters most all they make, but they have some for themselves. The Creek slaves do that way. They didn't have to stay on the master's place and work like the slaves of white people and the Cherokee and Choctaw people had to do.

Maybe my pappy and mammy run off and get free, or maybe-so they buy themselves out, but, anyway, they move away sometime, and my mammy's master sell me to old man Tuskaya-hini-ha when I was just a little girl.

I don't know where I been born. Nobody never did tell me. But my mammy and pappy got me after the war and I know then whose child I is. The men at the Creek Agency helped them get me.

First thing I remember, I belong to old Tuskaya-hiniha. He was a big man in the Upper Creek, and have a pretty good-size farm, just a little bit to the north of the wagon depot houses on the old road at Honey Springs, place about twenty-five miles south of Fort Gibson. The Elk River was about two miles north of where we lived; I know, because I been there many the time.

I don't know if Old Master have a white name. Lots of the

Upper Creek didn't have no white name. "Tuskaya-hiniha" means headman warrior in Creek. Everybody called him that, the family too.

My mistress's name was Nancy, and she was a Lott before she marry Tuskaya-hiniha. They have two chillun, but only one stayed on the place; she was named Luwina, and her husband was dead.

Luwina had a little baby boy and that the reason old Master buy me, to look after the baby. We called him "Istidji." That means little man.

Before the war, Old Master had about as many slaves as I got fingers. I can think them off on my fingers, like this, but I can't recollect the names. They called the slaves "istilusti." That means black man.

Tuskaya-hiniha was near blind before the war. About time of the war he go plumb blind and have to sit on the long seat under the brush shelter of the house. That about the time all the slaves begin to slip out and run off. Sometimes I lead him around the yard a little.

Old Master had a good log house and a brush shelter out in front like all the houses had. Like a gallery, only it had dirt for the floor and brush for the roof. They cooked everything out in the yard in big pots, and they ate out in the yard too.

That was sure good stuff to eat! Roast green corn on the ear in the ashes, and scrape off some and fry it. Grind the dry corn or pound it up and make ash cake. Then boil greens—all kinds of greens from out in the woods—and chop up pork and deer meat or wild turkey meat; maybe all of them in the big pot at the same time. Fish too, and turtle.

They always have a pot full of "sofki" right inside the house, and anybody eat when they feel hungry. Anybody come on a visit, always give them some of the sofki. If they don't take none, the old man get mad!

When you make sofki, you pound up corn real fine, then pour in water and drain it to get all the skin off the grain. You let the grits soak, then boil it, and let it stand. Sometime you put in some pounded hickory-nut meats.

I don't know where Old Master get the cloth for the clothes, unless he buy it. I think he had some slaves that weave the cloth, but when I was there, he got it at the wagon depot at Honey Springs. He go there all the time to sell his corn.

That place was on the big road, what we called the road to Texas. It go all the way up to the North too. The traders stop at Honey Springs and Old Master trade corn for what he want. He got some pretty checkedy cloth one time, and everybody got a dress or a shirt made off of it. I had that dress till I got too big for it.

◁ Cooking outdoors reduced the dangers of fire. The "winter kitchen," a separate, enclosed structure, stood well apart from the big house.

These Oklahoma slaves remembered traditional recipes of their Choctaw masters:

"One of our choicest was pashofa. We'd take corn and beat it in a mortar with a pestle. They took out the husks with a riddle—a kind of sifter. When it was beat fine enough to go through the riddle, we'd put it in a pot and cook it with fresh pork or beef." (Kiziah Love)

"Tom-budha was green corn and fresh meat cooked together and seasoned with tongue or pepper-grass." (Polly Colbert)

Everybody dress up fine when there is a funeral. The Creek sure take on when somebody die! Along in the night you wake up and hear a gun go off, way off yonder somewhere. Just as fast as they can ram the load in, again and again. The men go out in the yard and let the people know somebody dead that way. Then they go back in the house and let the fire go out. When somebody was sick, they build a fire in the house, even in the summer, and don't let it die down till that person get well or die. When they die, they let the fire go out.

In the morning everybody dress up fine and go to the house where the dead is and stand around in the yard outside. Don't go in. Pretty soon along come somebody what got a right to touch and handle the dead, and they go in. I don't know what give them the right. I think they has to go through some kind of medicine to get the right. I know they has to drink red root and purge good before they touch the body.

When they get ready, they come out and all go to the graveyard, mostly the family graveyard, right on the place or at some of the kinfolks'. They take me along to mind the baby.

When they get to the grave, somebody shoots a gun at the north, then the west, then the south, and then the east. If they had four guns they used them. They put the body down in the grave and put some extra clothes in with it and some food and a cup of coffee, maybe. Then they takes strips of elm bark and lays it over the body till it all covered up and then throw in the dirt.

When the last dirt throwed on, everybody must clap their hands and smile, but you sure hadn't better step on any of the new dirt around the grave, because it bring sickness back to your house right along with you.

Soon as the grave filled up, they built a little shelter over it with poles, like a pigpen, and cover it over with elm bark to keep the rain from soaking down in the new dirt. Then everybody go back to the house and the family go in and scatter some kind of medicine around the place and build a new fire. Sometime they feed everybody before they all leave for home.

Always a lot of the people say, "Didn't you hear the stikini squalling in the night?"

"I hear that stikini all the night!"

The "stikini" is the screech owl. He suppose to tell when anybody going to die right soon. Creek people say, hear the screech owl close to the house and sure enough somebody in the family die soon.

▽　　▽　　▽

When the big battle come at our place at Honey Springs, they just got through having the green corn "busk"—the green corn was ripe enough to eat. It must have been along in July.

That busk was just a little busk; there wasn't enough men around to have a good one. But I seen lots of big ones, where they had all the different kinds of "banga." They call all the dances some kind of banga. The chicken dance is the "tolosa-banga," and the "istifani-banga" is the one where they make like they is skeletons and raw heads coming to get you.

The "hadjo-banga" is the crazy dance, and that is a funny one. They all dance crazy and make up funny songs to go with the dance. Everybody whoop and laugh all the time.

The worst one was the drunk dance. They just dance ever whichaway, the men and the women together, and they wrassle and hug and carry on awful! Good people don't dance that one. Sometime the bad ones leave and go to the woods too!

That kind of doing make the good people mad, and sometime they have killings about it. When a man catch one of his women—maybeso his wife or one of his daughters—been to the woods, he cut off the rim of her ears.

People think that ain't so, but I know it is. I was combing somebody's hair one time—I ain't going to tell who—and when I lift it up off of her ears, I nearly drop dead. The rims cut right off of them! But she was a married woman, and I think maybe-so it happen when she was a young girl at one of them drunk dances.

Upper Creek took marrying kind of light, anyways. If the young'uns wanted to be man and wife, they just went ahead and that was about all, excepting some presents maybe. The Baptists changed that a lot.

I never forget the day that battle of the Civil War happen at Honey Springs! Old Master just had the green corn all in, and us had been having a time getting it in too. The women was all that was left, because the men slaves had slipped off and left out.

We had a big tree in the yard, and a grape vine swing in it for the little baby Istidji. I was swinging him real early in the morning. The house sat in a patch of woods with the field in the back, but out on the north side was an open space, like a prairie.

I was swinging the baby, and all at once I seen somebody riding across that prairie—just coming a-kiting and laying flat out on his horse. He begin to give the war whoop, "Eya-a-a-a-he-ah!" When he got close to the house, he holler to get out, because there going to be a big fight. Old Master start rapping with his cane and yelling to get grub and blankets in the wagon right now!

Some of the women run to get the mules and the wagon. Some start grabbing all the pots and kettles, getting meat and corn out of the place where we done hid it before now to keep the scouters from finding it. All the time, we hear that boy hollering. "Eya-a-a-he-he-hah!"

We leave everything right where it is, except putting out the fire. Then just as we starting, here come something across that prairie sure enough! We know they is Indians the way they is riding all strung out. They had a flag, and it was red and had a big crisscross on it. The wind whip it around the horse's head and the horse pitch and rear like he know something going happen, sure!

About that time it turn dark and begin to rain. We get out to the big road, and the rain come down hard. It rain so hard that we have to stop the wagon and just set there. Along come more soldiers than I ever see before. They all white, I think, and they have on that brown clothes dyed with walnut and butternut. Old Master say they Confederate soldiers. Most of the men slopping along in the rain on foot. They dragging some big guns on wheels.

Then we hear the fighting up to the north, where the river is, and the guns sound like horses loping across a plank bridge way off somewhere. The head men start hollering and some of the horses start rearing and the soldiers start trotting faster up the road. We can't get out on the road, so we strike off through the prairie and make for a creek that got high banks and a place on it we call Rocky Cliff.

We spend the whole day and that night in a big cave in that cliff, and listen to the battle going on. That was about half a mile from the wagon depot at Honey Springs, a little east of it. We can hear the guns going all day, and in the evening, here come the South making for a getaway. They come riding and running by where we is, and it don't make no difference how much the head men hollers at them, they can't make that bunch slow up and stop.

After a while here come the Yankees right after them, and they goes on into Honey Springs. Pretty soon we see the blaze where they is burning the wagon depot and the houses.

The next morning we goes back to the house and find the soldiers ain't hurt nothing much. The hogs is in the pen and the
chickens come cackling around. Them soldiers going so fast they
didn't have no time to stop and take nothing, I reckon.

Then along come the Yankee soldiers going back to the
North. They looks pretty wore out, but they is laughing and
joshing and going on.

Old Master pack up the wagon with everything he can carry
then. We strike out down the big road to get out of the way of
any more war, is they going to be any.

That old Texas road just crowded with wagons! Everybody
doing the same thing we is, and the rains made the road so
muddy and the soldiers tromp up the mud so bad that the wagons get stuck. The people all moving along in bunches. Every
little while one bunch of wagons come up with another bunch
stuck in the mud, and they put all the horses and mules on
together and pull them out, and then they go on together a
while.

At night they camp, and the women and what few Negroes
they is get the supper in the big pots. The men eat pretty nigh
everything up from the women and the Negroes.

After a while we come to the town Canadian. The South soldiers got in there ahead of us and took up all the houses to sleep
in. The next morning we leave that town and get to the big river
[the Canadian]. The rain make the river rise, and I never see so
much water! They got some boats we put the stuff on, and float
the wagons and swim the mules and finally get across, but it
look like we all going to drown.

Most the folks say they going to Boggy Depot and around
Fort Washita, but Old Master strike off by hisself and go way
down in the bottom to live. I don't know where it was, but there

been some kind of fighting around there, because we camp in houses and cabins nobody in them. Looks like the people got away quick, because all the stuff was in the houses, but you better scout around the house before you go up to it. Liable to be some scouters already in it! Them Indian soldiers quit the army and went scouting in bunches and took everything they find. If somebody tried to stop them, they got killed.

Sometime we find graves in the yard where somebody just been buried fresh. One house had some dead people in it when Old Mistress poke her head in. We get away from there, and no mistake!

By and by we find a little cabin and stop and stay. I was the only slave by that time. All the others done slip out and run off. We stay there two years, I reckon, because we make two little crops of corn. For meat, a man with us named Mr. Walker just went out in the woods and shoot the wild hogs. The woods was full of them wild hogs, and fish in the holes where he could sicken them with buck root and catch them with his hands—all we wanted.

I don't know when the war quit off, but I stayed with Tuskaya-hiniha long time after I was free, I reckon. I was just a little girl, and he didn't know where to send me to, anyways.

One day three men rode up and talked to the old man a while in English talk. Then he called and tell me to go with them to find my own family. He just laugh and slap my behind and set me up on the horse in front of one of the men, and they take me off and leave my good checkedy dress at the house!

We get to Canadian River again, and the men tie me on the horse so I can't fall off. There was all that water, and they ain't no bridge, and they ain't no boat, and we just swim the horses. I knowed sure I was going to be gone that time; but we got across.

▲ *Lucinda Davis, photographed at age 89 on the porch of her daughter's house. Her Creek master belonged to a tribe exiled to the Oklahoma Territory in 1838–39.*

When we come to the Creek Agency, there is my pappy and my mammy to claim me! I lived with them in the Verdigris [River] bottom above Fort Gibson, till I was grown. Then I married Anderson Davis at Gibson Station, and we got our allotments* on the Verdigris east of Tulsa—kind of south too, close to the town Broken Arrow.

I had lots of children, but only two is alive now. When my old man die, I come to live here with Josephine. I's blind and can't see nothing, and the noises in town pesters me. The children is all so ill-mannered. They holler at you, they don't mind you neither. When I could see and had my young'uns, I could just set in the corner and tell them what to do, because they was raised the old Creek way, and they know the old folks know the best.

* allotments: 160-acre parcels of land. The Oklahoma allotments were carved from traditional Indian lands. Early settlers in the Oklahoma Territory could claim or purchase these tracts if they promised to homestead them. Native Americans living in the Territory at the time of statehood, in 1907, were given first choice of the parcels, which they received free. Lucinda Davis's narrative suggests that her father may have been Creek, or part Creek, and he (and Lucinda) were entitled by blood, rather than by treaty, to their allotments.

Chapter 8
SAM MCALLUM

Sam McAllum, once a Mississippi slave, lived in
Meridian, Lauderdale County, in the 1930s. He was
born in 1842 and was probably about ninety-five at
the time of his interview.

The Stephenson plantation where I was born wasn't but
about thirteen miles north of DeKalb, in Kemper County.
My mammy belonged to the Stephensons, and my pappy
belonged to Marster Lewis Barnes. His plantation wasn't so very
far from Stephenson. My pappy was a old man when I was
born—I was the baby child. After he died, my mammy married
a McAllum Negro.

There were about thirty slaves at Stephenson. My mammy
worked in the field and her mammy, Lillie, was the yard woman.
She looked after the little colored chillun. The chillun would
play blind man, hiding, and whatever come to hand. I don't recollect any playthings us had, except a ball my young marster
gave me. He was Sam Lewis Stephenson, about my age.

My young marster learned me out of his speller, but Mistis

△ *Slave youngsters looked upon the plantation's cotton yard, the barns, shops, corn cribs, smokehouse, and streams as their playground.*

Home-made play equipment on the plantation:

"We chillun would slip a ax to the woods with us and make a flying mare to ride on. We would chop down a nice little pine tree so as there would be a good big stump left in the ground. Then we would chisel the top of the stump down all around the edges till we had us a right sharp peg setting up in the middle of the stump. After that was fixed, we would cut us another pole a little bit smaller than that one and bore a hole in the middle of it to make it set down on that peg.

"One of us chillun would get on this end and another one would get on the other end, and us chillun would give them a shove that would send them flying around fast as I could say mighty-me-a-life. Everybody would be crazy to ride on the flying mare. All the neighbors' chillun would gather up and go in the woods and jump and shout about which one turn come to ride next.

"Them was big pleasures us had in that day and time, and they never cost nobody nothing neither." (Lizzie Davis, South Carolina) whipped me. She said I didn't need to learn nothing except how to count, so I could feed the mules without colicking them. You gave them ten ears of corn to the mule. If you gave them more, it would colic them and they'd die. They cost more than a Negro would. That was the first whipping I ever got—when me and my young marster were a-spelling.

I stayed with him special, but I waited on all the white folks' chillun at Stephenson. I carried the foot tub in at night and washed their feet, and I'd pull the trundle bed out from under the other bed. All the boys slept in the same room.

Then I was a yard boy and waited on the young marster and mistis. Hadn't been to the field then—hadn't worked yet.

Mr. Stephenson was a surveyor, and he fell out with Mr. McAllum and had a lawsuit. He [Stephenson] had to pay it in darkies. Mr. McAllum had the privilege of taking me and my mammy, or another woman and her two. He took us. So us come to the McAllum plantation to live. It was in Kemper too, about eight miles from Stephenson. Us come there during the war. That was when my mammy married one of the McAllum Negroes.

My new pappy went to the war with Mr. McAllum and was with him when he was wounded at Manassas Gap battle. He brung him home to die—and he done it.

The Yankees come through DeKalb, hunting up cannons and guns and mules. They sure did eat a heap. Us hid all the best things like silver, and drove the stock to the swamp. I was plowing a mule and the Yankees made me take him out. They didn't burn nothing, but us heard tell of burnings in Scooba and Meridian.

Times were tight—not a grain of coffee and not much else. When our clothes wore plumb out, the mistis and the Negro women made us some out of the cotton us had raised. My granny stayed in the loom room all the time. The other women done the spinning and she done the weaving. She was a good'n.

The M&O [Mobile & Ohio Railroad] was burning wood then. They couldn't get coal. They used tallow pots instead of oil. The engineer had to climb out on the engine hisself and tend to them tallow pots. They do different now.

Mistis didn't have nobody to help her during the war. She had to do the best she could. When she heard the Negroes talking about being free, she wore them out with a cowhide. She wasn't a powerful-built woman neither. She had to do it herself, because 'twasn't nobody to do it for her. There was such a scarcity of men, they were putting them in the war at sixty-five.

Some folks treated their slaves mighty bad, put dogs on them. All my white folks were good to their slaves, according to how good they behaved theirselves. Course, you couldn't leave no plantation without a pass or the patteroller'd get you. I ain't counting that, because that was something everybody knowed beforehand.

There was a heap of talk about the Yankees giving every Negro forty acres and a mule. I picked out my mule. All of us did. Never got none of it.

Times were mighty tough. Us thought us knowed trouble during the war. Um-m-m! Us didn't know nothing about trouble. There were so many slaves at McAllum's, they had to thin them out. Mistis put us out [hired out her slaves for wages, to be paid to herself]. She sent me to Mr. Scott, close to Scooba. I was almost a grown boy by then and could plow pretty good.

Come the Surrender, Mr. Scott said, "Sambo, I don't have to pay your mistis for you no more. Negroes is free. I have to pay you if you stay. You is free."

I didn't believe it. I worked that crop out, but I didn't ask for no pay. I didn't understand about Freedom, so I went home to my old mistis. She said, "Sambo, you don't belong to me now."

▲ *Hauling vegetables from the garden. Slave children learned to carry progressively heavier loads in preparation for work in the field.*

They bound us young Negroes out. They sent me and my brother to a man that was going to give us some learning along with farming. His name was Overstreet. Us ain't never seen no speller nor nothing [at Overstreet's], but us worked that crop out. My mammy and me went back to McAllum's and stayed until a man give us a patch in return for us helping him on his farm.

I know about the Ku Kluxes. I seen them. Ain't nobody know exactly about them Ku Kluxes. But folks that ain't acted right liable to be found tied up somewheres. The Negroes were having a party one Saturday night on Hampton's plantation. Come some men on horses with some kind of scare face on them. They were all wrapped up, disguised; the horses were covered up too.

They called for Miler Hampton. He was one of the Hampton Negroes. He been up to something; they said he done something bad. They carried him off with them and killed him that very night. They didn't have no trouble getting him, because us were all scared us'd get killed too.

Us went to DeKalb next day in a drove and asked the white folks to help us. Us buy all the ammunition us could get, because us were having another party the next week. They didn't come to that party.

Then I go to work for Mr. Ed McAllum in DeKalb—when I ain't working for the Gullys. When the Curries come to Meridian to live, they give me charge of their plantation. I was the leader and stayed and worked the plantation for them. They been living in Meridian twelve years. I was married by this time to Laura. She was the nursemaid to Mr. J. H. Currie. She's been dead twenty years. I's married now to their cook.

Mr. Hector told me if I'd come and live with them here, he'd give me this house here in the backyard and paint it and fix it all up. It's mighty pleasant in the shade. Folks used to always set their houses in a grove, but now they cut down more trees than they keep. Us don't cut no trees. Us porches is always nice and shady.

I've got four boys living. One son was in the big strike in the automobile plant in Detroit and couldn't come to see me last Christmas. He'll come to see me next year, if I'm still here.

Chapter 9
CHARLEY MITCHELL

*Charley Mitchell was eighty-five when interviewed in
Panola County, Texas. Most slaves labored on farms
or plantations; Mitchell's account tells of his life
as a city slave.*

I was born in Virginia, over in Lynchburg, and it was in 1852.
I belonged to Parson Terry and Missy Julia. I don't remember
my pappy, because he was sold when I was a baby, but my
mammy was willed to the Terrys and always lived with them till
Freedom. She worked for them and they hired her out there in
town for cook and house servant.

They hired me out most times as nurse for white folks'
chillun, and I nursed Tom Thurman's chillun. He run the bakery there in Lynchburg and come from the North, and when
war broke, they made him and another Northerner take an
iron-clad oath they wouldn't help the North.

I didn't get no schooling. The white folks always said Negroes
don't need no learning. Some Negroes learnt to write their ini-
tials on the barn door with charcoal. They try to find out who

done that, the white folks, I mean, and say they cut his fingers off if they just find out who done it.

During the war I worked in Massa Thurman's bakery, helping make hardtack and doughnuts for the Confederate soldiers. He give me plenty to eat and wear and treated me as well as I could hope for.

Lynchburg was good sized when war come on and Woodruff's Negro trading yard was about the biggest thing there. It was all fenced in and had a big stand in the middle of where they sold the slaves. They got a big price for them and handcuffed and chained them together and led them off like convicts. That yard was full of Louisiana and Texas slave buyers most all the time. None of the Negroes wanted to be sold to Louisiana, because that's where they beat them till the hide was raw, and salted them and beat them some more.

Of course, us slaves of white folks what lived in town wasn't treated like they was on most plantations. Massa Nat and Missy Julia was good to us, and most the folks we was hired out to was good to us. Lynchburg was full of patterollers just like the country, though, and they had a fenced-in whipping post there in town and the patterollers sure put it on a Negro if they catch him without a pass.

▽ *Slave pass. Slaves had to get a dated permit to go off the owner's property—a peril even with a pass, and a hardship for husbands and wives living on separate plantations.*

▲ *Poor roads everywhere isolated country dwellers, and made any travel special. Few persons passing the plantation on foot went unnoticed.*

After war broke, Lee—General Lee himself—come to Lynchburg and had a campground there. It looked like another town. General Shumaker was commander of the Confederate artillery and killed the first Yankee that come to Lynchburg. The Confederates had a scrimmage with the Yankees about two miles out from Lynchburg, and after Surrender, General Wilcox and a company of Yankees come there.

The camp was close to a big college there in Lynchburg, and they throwed up a breastworks out the other side the college. They drilled the college boys there in town. I didn't know till after Surrender what they drilled them for, because the white folks didn't talk the war amongst us.

About a year after the Yankees come to Lynchburg, they moved the colored free school out to Lee's camp and met in one of the barracks, and had four white teachers from the North. That school run several years after Surrender.

▷ *Illiterate slaves understood the power of education. After Freedom, they seized the chance to get their children— and themselves—schooled.*

This former slave savored what Freedom brought her and her descendents:

"Lots of old people like me say that they was happy in slavery and that they had the worst tribulations after Freedom, but I knows they didn't have no white master and overseer like we all had on our place. They both dead now, I reckon, and there's no use talking about the dead, but I know I been gone long ago if that white man Saunder didn't lose his hold on me.

"Maybe they that kind still yet, but they don't show it up no more, and I got lots of white friends too. All my chillun and grandchillun been to school, and they get along good, and I know we living in a better world. I sure thank the good Lord I got to see it." (Katie Rowe, Oklahoma)

Lots of Confederate soldiers passed through Lynchburg going to Petersburg. Once some Yankee soldiers come through close by and there was a scrimmage between the two armies, but it didn't last long. General Wilcox had a standing army in Lynchburg after the war, when the Yankees took things over, but everything was peaceful and quiet then.

After Surrender, a man calls a meeting of all the slaves in the fairgrounds and tells us we was free. We wasn't promised anything. We just had to do the best we could. We had to go to work for whatever they'd pay us. We didn't have nothing when we was turned loose and no place to go but down the street and road. I heared lots of slaves what lived on farms say they was promised forty acres and a mule; but they never did get it.

When I left the Terrys, I worked in a tobacco factory for a dollar a week. That was big money to me. Mammy worked too, and we managed somehow to live.

After I married I started farming, but since I got too old, I live around with my chillun. I have two sons and a boy what I raised. One boy lives close to Jacksonville and the other in the Sabine bottom, and the boy what I raised lives at Henderson.

Chapter 10

FRANKIE GOOLE

The mother of this former Tennessee slave sought legal
help to get custody of her daughter at the time
of Freedom.

I was born in Smith County on the other side of Lebanon. I'll
be eighty-five years old Christmas Day.

My old missus was named Sallie, and my marster was George
Waters. My mammy's name was Lucindia. She was sold from
me when I was six weeks old, and my missus raised me. I always
slept with her. My missus was good to me, but my marster—her
son—whipped me.

I used to drive up the cows and my feet would be so cold and my
toes cracked open and bleeding. I'd be crying till I got almost to the
house. Then I'd wipe my eyes on the bottom of my dress, so the
marster wouldn't know that I had been crying.

When the Negroes was freed, all of my missus's slaves slipped
away, except me. One morning she told me to go down and wake
them up.

I went down and knocked. Nobody said nothing.

I pushed on the door. It come open, and I fell in the room. I went back to Missus.

She said, "What is the matter with you?"

I said, "I pushed on the door and hurt my chin. Uncle John and all of them is gone."

She said, "You know they is not gone. Go back and get them up."

I had to go back, but they weren't there.

I remember the Ku Klux Klan and patterollers. They would come around and whip the Negroes with a bullwhip. I's stood in our door and heard the hard licks and screams.

I'd tell my missus, "Listen to that!"

She would say, "See, that is what will happen to you if you try to leave."

After Freedom, my mammy come from Lebanon and got me. I'll never forget that day—oh Lordy! I can see her now. My old missus's daughter-in-law had got a bunch of switches to whip me. I was standing in the door shaking all over, and the young

TAKEN UP

AND committed to the jail of Bexar County, Texas, on the 13th day of March, 1854, a negro man, calling himself MARTIN, or TOM. He says he is a blacksmith, and belongs to John Beal, Attakapas, on Red River. Said negro is about 48 years of age, 5 feet 8 or 9 inches high, and head a little bald. His back is marked with the whip, and marks of cupping on both temples and back of the neck. He speaks Creole French and broken English. The owner of said negro is hereby notified forward, prove property, pay and take him away, or he will with as the law directs.
W. B. KNOX, Sheriff
By L. SARGENT,

◁ *"Marster would tell the overseer, 'Don't you cut my Negro's hide or scar him,' because the buyers would see the scars and say that he was a bad Negro." (Isaiah Green, Georgia)*

▽ *A classified ad. As early as the 1700s, newspapers printed the symbol of a running figure to advertise the reward for capture of a runaway.*

RUNAWAY NEGROES.

TAKEN up and committed to the Jail of Rowan county, on the 7th day of January, two negro men, Prince and June. Prince is about 30 years of age, 5 feet 5 inches high. June is about 35 years old, 5 feet high, and say they belong to John D. A. Murphy, of Lexington District, South Carolina. The owner is requested to come forward, prove property, pay charges and take them away.
NOAH ROBERTS, Jailor.
Jan 11, 1845   tf 37

missus was telling me to get my clothes off.

I said, "I seed a woman coming through the gate."

My missus said, "That is Lucindia!" and the young missus hid the switches.

My mammy said, "I's come to get my child."

My missus told her to let me spend the night with her, then she'd send me to the courthouse at nine o'clock next morning. So I stayed with the missus that night. She told me to always be a good girl, and don't let a man or boy trip me. I didn't know what she meant, but I always remembered what she said.

I went to the courthouse and met my mammy. The courtroom was jammed with people. The judge told me to hold my right hand up. I was so scared I stuck both hands up.

Judge said, "Frankie, is that your mammy?"

I said, "I don't know. She says she is." What did I know of a mammy that was took from me at six weeks old?

He said, "Was your marster good to you?"

I said, "My missus was, but my marster wasn't. He whipped me."

He said to my mammy, "Lucindia, take this child and be good to her, for she has been mistreated. Someday she can make a living for you."

And thank the Lord, I did keep her in her old days and was able to bury her.

When I left out of the courtroom, different people gave me money, and I had my hat almost full. That was the only money I had given to me. My missus didn't give me nothing except my clothes in a carpetbag.

The first pair of shoes I ever had was after I come to Nashville. They had high tops. I had some red-striped socks with them. I guess I was about twelve years old when my mammy brought me to Nashville and put me to work. I nursed Miss

Sadie Pope Fall; she married Mat Gardner. I also nursed Miss Sue Porter Houston. I went to school one year at Fisk in the year 1869.

I belong to the Baptist Church. The colored people used to have camp meetings, and they'd last for two weeks. Lord have mercy, did we have a time at them meetings—preaching, singing, and shouting. Some of them would shout till their throats would be sore. And over somewhere near they would be cooking mutton and different good things to eat.

Oh Lordy, how they did baptize down at the wharf! The people would gather at the wharf on the first Sunday in May. They would come from all the Baptist churches. Would leave the church singing and shouting and keep that up till they got to the river. These last few years they have got too stylish to shout.

The last man I worked for was at the Link Hotel. Then I started

◁ *"Marster loved to come out on Sundays to see us chillun get our heads combed. Honey, there was sure hollering when they started working on us."* (Lina Hunter, Georgia)

The Civil War's end reunited slave families:

"Soon as my daddy hear them firing off for the Surrender, he put out for the plantation where he first belong, to get me and carry me home with him.

"My mistis, she say, 'Stay here with me and I'll give you a school learning.'

"Then my daddy say, 'She has to go with me. Her mama told me not to come home without her.'

"I never will forget riding behind my daddy on that mule way in the night. Us left in such a hurry I didn't get none of my clothes, hardly, and I ain't seed my mistis from that day to this!" (Cheney Cross, Alabama)

keeping boarders—have fed all these Nashville police. The police is the ones that helped get these relief orders for me. I lived twenty-two years where the Hermitage Laundry is. That is where I got the name Mammy: While living there I raised eighteen chillun, white and black; and some of them is good to me now. I have lived on this street for sixty years.

I remember when the yellow fever and the cholera was here, in 1870 and 1873. They didn't have coffins enough to put them in, so they used boxes and piled the boxes in wagons like hauling wood.

I had some papers about my age and different things, but when the backwaters got up, they got lost. I didn't have to move; I kept praying and talking to the Lord and I believe he heard me, for the water didn't get in my house.

This young people, oh, my Lord, they ain't worth talking about, they drink whiskey—I call it Old Bust Head—and do such mean things. I try to shame these women, I's disgusted at my own color. They try to know too much and don't know nothing; and they don't work enough.

When it comes to working, I ain't worth a dime now, for I ain't able to do nothing. I can't complain of my living, though, since the relief has been taking care of me.

Chapter 11
ELLEN BETTS

Ellen Betts's grandparents and their masters came
from Virginia and settled in Louisiana about 1853.
She was eighty-four and living in Texas at the time of
her interview, where she moved sometime after
Freedom. Her interviewer writes: "Ellen lives with
friends who support her. Her sole belonging is an old
trunk, and she carries the key on a string
around her neck."

I got borned on the Bayou Teche, close to Opelousas, in St. Mary's Parish. I belonged to Tolas Parsons, who had about five hundred slaves, counting the little ones. When my eyes just barely fresh open, Marse Tolas died and willed the whole lot of us to his brother, William Tolas.

Marse William was the greatest man ever walked this earth, that's the truth. When a whipping got to be done, Old Marse do it himself. He don't allow no overseer to throw his gals down and pull up their dress and whip on their bottoms like I hear tell some of them do. Was he still living, I expect one part of his hands be with him today. I know I would.

Aunt Rachel, what cooked in the big house for Miss Cornelia, had four young'uns, and them chillun fat and slick. Marse sure proud them black, slick chillun. All the Negroes had to stoop to Aunt Rachel, just like they curtsy to Missy.

Marse William have the prettiest place up and down that bayou, with the house and fine trees and such. From where we live, it's five mile to Centerville one way, and five mile to Patterson the other. They haul lumber from one place or the other to make wood houses for the slaves. Sometime Marse buy furniture and sometime the carpenter make it.

Miss Sidney was Marse's first wife and he had six boys by her. Then he marry the widow Cornelia and she give him four boys. With ten chillun springing up quick like that and all the colored chillun coming along fast as pig litters, I don't do nothing all my days but nurse, nurse, nurse. When the colored women had to cut cane all day till midnight come and after, I had to nurse the babies for them and tend the white chillun too. I nurse so many chillun it done went and stunted my growth, and that's why I ain't nothing but bones to this day.

Some of them was so fat and big I had to tote their feet while another gal tote their head. The big folks leave a toddy for colic and crying and such. I done drink the toddy and let the chillun have the milk. I don't know no better, I was such a little one, about seven or eight years old. It's a wonder I ain't the biggest drunkard in this here country, counting all the toddy I done put in my young belly!

When late of night come, if them babies wake up and bawl, I set up a screech and out-screech them till they shut their mouth. The louder they bawl, the louder I bawl. Sometime when Marse hear the babies cry, he come down and say, "Why the chillun cry like that, Ellen?"

I say, "Marse, I get so hungry and tired I done drink the milk up."

△ *What slave children wore sometimes identified the plantation they belonged to. Shirts and dresses cut from the same bolt clothed them in a uniform.*

Child care on small plantations:

"My mammy was a plow hand, and she'd put me under the shade of a big old post-oak tree and go to work. There I sat all day, and that tree was my nurse. It still standing there yet, and I won't let nobody cut it down." (Oliver Bell, Alabama)

"Old Miss would fix my bread and licker in a tin lid and shove it to me on the floor. I never ate at the table until I was twelve, and that was after Freedom." (Sarah Douglas, Arkansas)

When I talk sassy like that, Marse just shake his finger at me, because he knowed I's a good one and don't let no little mite starve.

Nobody ever hit me a lick. Marse always said being mean to the young'uns made them mean when they grew up. Marse have the house girls make popcorn for them, and candy. Marse don't even let the chillun go to the big cane patch. He plant little bitty patches close to the house and each have a patch and work it till it got growed.

I nurse the sick folks too. Sometimes I dosed with Blue Mass pills [popular medicine of the time, containing mercury], and sometimes Doc Fawcett leave rhubarb and ipecac and calomel and castor oil and such. Two years after the war, I got married and got chillun of my own, and then I turned into the wet nurse. I wet nurse the white chillun and black chillun, like they all the same color. Sometimes I have a white one pulling on one side and a black one the other.

I wanted to get the papers for midwifing, but law, I don't never have no time for learning in slave time. If Marse catch a paper in your hand, he sure whip you. He don't allow no bright Negroes around; he sell them quick. He always say, "Book learning don't raise no good sugarcane." The only learning he allowed was when they learn the colored chillun the Methodist catechism. The only writing a Negro ever got was when he got born or married or died. Then Marse put the name in the big book.

I recollect the time Marse marry Miss Cornelia. He went on the mail boat and brung her from New Orleans. She the prettiest woman in the world almost, excepting she have the biggest mouth I nearly ever seed. He brung her to the house and all the Negroes and boys and girls and cats and dogs and such come

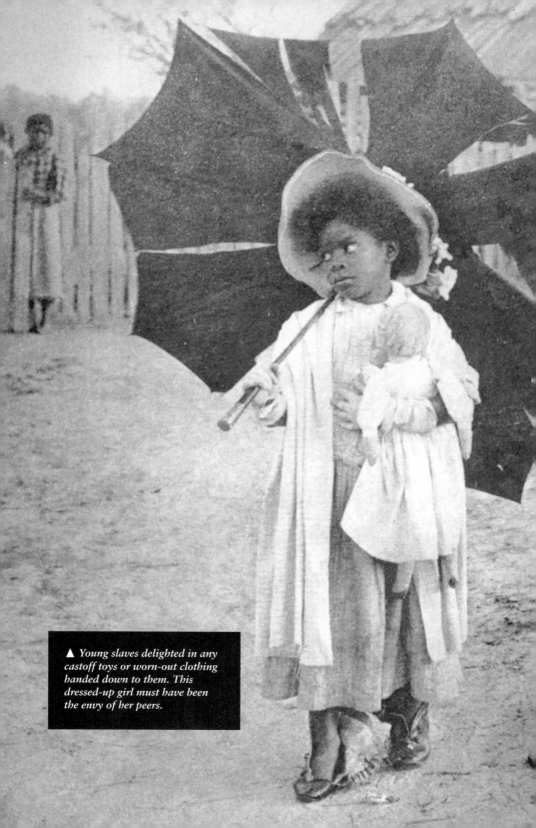

▲ *Young slaves delighted in any castoff toys or worn-out clothing handed down to them. This dressed-up girl must have been the envy of her peers.*

and salute her. There she stand on the gallery, with a pretty white dress on with red stripes running up and down.

Marse say to her, "Honey, see all the black folks? They belong to you now."

She wave to us and smile on us, and the next day she give her wedding dress to my ma. That the finest dress I ever seen. It was purple and green silk; and all the Negro gals wear that dress when they got married. My sister Sidney wore it, and Sary and Mary.

Miss Cornelia was the finest woman in the world. Come Sunday morning, she put a bucket of dimes on the front gallery and stand there and throw dimes to the chillun, just like feeding chickens. I'm right here to testify, because I was right there helping grab.

Sometimes she put the washtub of buttermilk on the back gallery and us chillun bring us gourds and dip up that good old buttermilk till it all got drunk up. Sometimes she fetch bread and butter to the back gallery and pass it out when it don't even come mealtime.

Miss Cornelia set my ma to cutting patterns and sewing right away. She give the women a bolt of linsey to make clothes and Ma cut the pattern. Us all have fine drawers down to the ankle, buttoned with pretty white buttons on the bottom.

Ma sure cut a mite of drawers, with sewing for her eleven gals and four boys too. In the summertime, we got a bolt of blue cloth and white tape for trimming, to make Sunday dresses. For the field, the Negroes got homespun, that you make jumpers out of. Marse say, "Don't go into the field dirty Monday morning. Scrub yourself and put on the clean jumper."

Marse sure good to them gals and bucks what cutting the cane. When they got done making sugar, he give a drink called "peach 'n' honey" to the womenfolk and whiskey and brandy to the men. Of all the dancing and capering! My pa was fiddler and we'd cut the pigeon wing, and cut the buck, and every other kind of dance. Sometimes Pa got tired and say he ain't going to play no more; and us gals got busy and pop him corn and make candy, so to entice him to play more.

I seen thousands and thousands of sugar barrels and kettles of syrup in my day. Marse sure turn over in his grave, did he know about some of that molasses. Them black boys don't care. I seen them pull rats out of the sugar barrel; they taste the sugar and say, "Ain't nothing wrong with that sugar. It's still sweet." One day a pert one pull a dead scorpion out of the syrup kettle. He just laugh and say, "Marse don't want to waste none of this syrup," and he lick the syrup right off that scorpion's body and legs.

Lord knows how much cane Old Marse have. To them that work hour in, hour out, them sugarcane fields sure stretch from

▽ In the cane, cotton, and tobacco fields, women slaves had to "keep up their row" and produce as much work as the men slaves did.

one end of the earth to the other. Marse ship hogs and hogs of sugar down the bayou. I seen the riverboats go down with big signs that say "Buy This Here Molasses" on the side. And he raise a world of rice and potatoes and corn and peanuts too.

When the work slight, us black folks have the balls and dinners and such. We get all day to barbecue meat down on the bayou, and the white folks come down and eat alongside of the colored.

When a black gal marry, Marse marry her hisself in the big house. He marry them Saturday, so they get Sunday off too. One time the riverboat come bearing the license for Negroes to get married with. Marse chase them off and say: "Don't you come trucking no papers around my Negroes. When I marry them, they marry as good as if the Lord God hisself marry them, and it don't take no paper to bind the tie."

Marse don't stand no messing around neither. A gal have to be of age and ask her pa and ma and Marse and Missy; and if they agree, they go ahead and get marry. Marse have the marry book to put the name down.

One time Marse take me along to help tote some chillun. He done write up to Virginny for to buy fresh hands. There was a old man that hobbled along the wagon and the chillun start to throw rocks.

The old man turn around to one prissy one and say, "Go on, young'un, you'll be where dogs can't bark at you tomorrow."

Next morning, us cooking in the kitchen, and all a sudden that little boy just crumple up dead on the floor. Law, we's scared. Nobody ever bother that old man no more, for he sure lay the evil finger on you.

Marse's brother, Conrad, a widowman, come to live on the plantation, and he had a little gal about eight years old. One

day she in the plum orchard playing with a rattlesnake and
Marse Conrad have a fit. The little gal won't let nobody hurt
that snake and she play with him. He won't bite her. She keeps
him about three years, and she'd rub and grease him. One day
he get sick and they give him some brandy, but he die, and Old
Doc pickled him in the bottle of brandy. That gal got so full of
grief, they take her to the infirmary in New Orleans, and then
one day she up and die.

That snake ain't all what Doc Fawcett pickle. A slave woman
give birth to a baby gal what have two faces with a strip of hair
running between. Doc Fawcett pickle it in the jar of brandy.

One day a man come riding by on a little dun horse so fast
you couldn't see that horse's tail a-switching. He whooping and
hollering. Us begun whoop and holler too. Then first thing you
know, the Yanks and the Democrats begun to fight. The war
met right there, and them Yanks and Democrats fought for
twenty-four hours straight running. There's a high old mountain in front of Marse's house, and the Yanks pepper cannon-
balls down from the top of that hill.

When the bullets start raining down, Marse call us and slip us
way back into the woods where it's so black and deep. Next day,
when the fight over, Marse come out with great big wagons piled
full of mess-poke for us to eat. That what us call hot meat. Us
sure glad to escape from the Yankees.

When us drove back to the plantation, seen a sight I never
seen. Them Yanks have killed men and women. I seed babies
picked up from the road with their brains bust right out. One old
man was drawing water and a cannonball shoots him right in
the well. They draws him up with the fishing line. There's a old
sugar boat out on the bayou with blood and sugar running
alongside the busted barrels. Molasses run in the bayou, and

blood run in the ditches. Marse have a great big orchard on the road and it wipe clean as a whistle. Bullets wipe up everything and bust that sugarcane all to pieces. The house sat far back and escape the bullets; but law, the time they have!

There's awful, awful times after that. A old cotton dress cost five dollars and a pound of coffee cost five dollars and a pint cup of flour cost six bits. Yanks was around all the time, and one day they come right in the house where Miss Cornelia was eating her dinner. They march around the table, just scooping up meat and potatoes and grabbing corn pone right and left. Miss Cornelia don't say a word, just smile sweet as honey cake. I reckon them soldiers might a took the silver and such only she charm them by being so quiet and ladylike. First thing you know, them soldiers curtsy to Missy and take themself right out the door and don't come back.

Then it seem like Marse have all the trouble in the world. His boy Ned die in the war, and William, named for his pa, drink bad all the time.

After the war, them Ku Kluxers that wear false faces try to tinker with Marse's Negroes. One day Uncle Dave start to town and a Kluxer ask him where he pass. That Kluxer clout him, but Uncle Dave outrun him in the cane.

Marse a judge and he make that man pay the fine for hitting Uncle Dave. After they hears of that, them old poky faces scared of Old Marse and they got out from Opelousas and stays out.

When Emancipation come, Marse got on the big block and say, "You all is as free as I is, standing right here. Does you want to stay with me, you can, and I'll pay you for the work."

All the Negroes cheer and say they want to stay, but Marse die not long after and us scatter.

I sure recollect that day Old Marse die. He keep saying,

"Where's Charity? Tell Charity to come."

They fetched Ma from the cane patch and she hold Marse's hand till he die. Us went to the graveyard and us sure cry over Old Marse.

When me and my husband, John, come to Texas, the folks say that Louisiana masters the meanest in the world. I say right back at them that there is good and mean in every spot of the earth. What's more, the Louisiana masters free their Negroes a year before any Texas Negro got free.

Law, times ain't like they was in slave days. All my ten chillun is dead and my old man gone, and now I reckon my time's about arrive. All I got to do now is pray the Lord to keep me straight. Then when the great day come, I can march the road to glory.

Chapter 12
MAGGIE WESMOLAND

Maggie Wesmoland was about thirteen years old when the Civil War ended; eighty-five when interviewed in the 1930s at Brinkley, Arkansas.

I was born in Arkansas in slavery time beyond Des Arc. My mother was Jane Holland, and my father was Smith Woodson. They lived on different places here in Arkansas. She was Mrs. Holland's cook and wash woman. The Hollands raised me and my sister. I was give to Mrs. Holland's daughter. She was my young mistress. She married a Cargo. He was a middle-age man, but Miss Betty Holland was in her teens.

I never seed my father after the closing of the war. He had been refugeed to Texas and come back here, then he went on to Mississippi. Mama had seventeen chillun. She had six by my stepfather. When my stepfather was mustered out at De Valls Bluff, he come to Mrs. Holland's and got Mama and took her on with him. I never seen Mama after she left.

I had a hard time. I was awfully abused by the old man that married Miss Betty. He was a poor man, never been used to

Know all men By these presents that I Jesse
Perkins Ser. of Caswell County and St. of N. Carolina
for and in consideration of the love Goodwill and
affection which I have and do bear towards my
Loving Daughter Rachel King Widow of the County
and State above Written have given and granted
and By these presents do freely give and grant
unto the said Rachel King A Negro Girl about Ten
years old of a yellow Complexion Named Clary and her
Increase to her the Sd Rachel King her lifetime and
at her death to be Equally Divided between her
three Children Nancy King Sealy King and Samuel
King which before the signing of these presents
I have Delivered her the Sd Rachel King this said girl
above named to have and to hold her lifetime as her own
Property free from the Claim or Claims of me or any
other person or persons whatever In witness whereof
I have hereunto set my hand and fixt my
Seal this the 11th of October 1814

Test
William Morgan Jur.

Jesse Perkins (seal)

Wm King (mark)

△ *Deed of gift. Slaveowners routinely gave each of their children a young slave as a personal servant. The gift of a slave couple ("a start of slaves") was a conventional wedding present.*

nothing and took spite on me everything happened. I was scared to death of him—he beat me so. He kept a bundle of hickory switches at the house. He never had been used to Negroes, and he didn't like them. I'm scarred up all over now where he lashed me. The flies blowed me time and again. Miss Betty, catch him gone, would grease my places and put turpentine on them to kill the places blowed.

I never did know what suit him and what wouldn't. Didn't nothing please him. I had to go in a trot all the time. One time the cow kicked over my milk. I was scared not to take some milk to the house, so I went to the spring and put water in the milk. He was snooping round somewhere and seen me. He beat me nearly to death.

▽ *Indoor plumbing was unknown. To slave children fell the chore of fetching the household water from the nearest stream, pond, well, or pump.*

He wouldn't buy me shoes. Miss Betty would have, but in them days the man was head of his house. The ice cut my feet. Miss Betty made me moccasins to wear—made them out of old rags and pieces of his pants. I had frostbite and risings on my feet till they was solid sores. Miss Betty, catch him out of sight, would doctor my feet. Seem like she was scared of him. He wasn't none too good to her.

When Miss Betty Holland married Mr. Cargo, she lived close to Dardanelle in the deer and bear hunting country. That is where he was so mean to me. Two men come there every year. They visited him every spring and fall, hunting deer.

He was a biggity-acting and braggy-talking old man. He whipped me twice before them deer hunters. They knowed he was showing off. One time he beat me before them, and on their way home, they went to the Freedmen's Bureau and told how he beat me and what he done it for—biggetness.

Good while after Freedom, a couple or three years, he went to town to buy them some things for Christmas. When he got to town, they asked him if he wasn't hiding a little Negro girl, asked if he sent me to school.

I slept on a bed made down at the foot of their bed. He come home that night, he told what all they ask him and what all he said. He told his wife the Freedmen's Bureau said turn that Negro girl loose.

She didn't want me to leave her. He said he would kill whoever come there bothering about me. He been telling that about.

He told Miss Betty they would fix me up and let me go stay a week at my sister's, Christmas. I hadn't seen my sister in about four years.

Miss Betty made the calico dress for me and made a body out of some of his pants legs and quilted the skirt part, bound it at the bottom with red flannel. She made my things nice—put my underskirt in a little frame and quilted it, so it would be warm. He went back to town, bought me the first shoes I had had since they took me. They was brogan shoes. They put a pair of his socks on me.

Christmas day was a bright warm day. In the morning, when Miss Betty dressed me up, I was so proud. He started me off and told me how to go. It was nearly twenty-five miles. Mr. Cargo told me if I wasn't back at his house New Year's Day, he would come after me on his horse and run me every step of the way home. He said he would give me the worst whipping I ever got in my life.

I got to the big creek. I got down in the ditch—couldn't get across. I was running up and down it, looking for a place to cross. A big old mill was up on the hill. I could see it. I seen three men coming, a white man with a gun and two Negro men on horses or mules. I heard one say, "Yonder she is."

Another said, "It don't look like her."

"Call her."

One said, "Margaret."

I answered. They come to me and said, "Go to the mill and cross on a foot log."

I went up there and crossed and got up on a stump behind my brother-in-law on his horse. One of them fellows what come for me had been to Cargo's and seen me. He was the Negro man, come to show Patsy's husband and his sharecropper where I was at. The white man was the man he was sharecropping with. They all lived close together in a big yard, like.

When New Year's Day come, I was going back, scared not to be back. Had no other place to live. The white man locked me up in a room in his house, and I stayed in there two days. They brought me plenty to eat. I slept in there with their chillun.

This white man bound me to his wife's friend for a year to keep Mr. Cargo from getting me back. It was Mrs. Brown, twenty miles from Dardanelle, they bound me over to. I never got no more than the common run of Negro children, but they wasn't mean to me. I missed my whippings! I never got none that whole year! The woman at the house and Mr. Cargo nearly had war about me.

It started in raining and cold and the roads was bad. Mr. Cargo never come after me till March. He didn't see me when he come. I seen him. I had been in the woods getting sweet gum when I seen him. He scared me. I lay down and covered up in leaves. They was deep. He never seen me.

Four or five years after I left there, he overtook me on a horse one day. I was grown. I was on my way from school. He said Miss Betty wanted to see me so bad, wanted me to come back and live with them. He wanted to come get me a certain day.

I lied about where I lived. I was so scared I lied and said yes to all he said. I was afraid to meet him on the road. He went to the wrong place to get me, I heard.

He died at Dardanelle before I come 'way from there.

I can't tell you to save my life what a hard time I had when I was growing up. I worked in the field a mighty little, but I have done a mountain of washing and ironing in my life. After I got grown, I hired out cooking at $1.25 a week and then $1.50 a week.

Conditions is far better for young folks now than when I come on. They can get chances I couldn't get. We own our house. My daughter is a blessing to me. She is so good to me. Times is all right if I was able to work.

A SELECTED READING LIST
ON VARIOUS ASPECTS OF SLAVERY

The original manuscripts of *Slave Narratives: A Folk History of Slavery in the U.S. from Interviews with Former Slaves* can be read by people of any age. Multivolume editions of the collection in facsimile have been published, one by Scholarly Press, St. Clair Shores, Michigan, 1976; another, *The American Slave: A Composite Autobiography,* George P. Rawick, editor, by Greenwood Press, Westport, Connecticut, 1972. Rawick's edition includes narratives from Fisk University interviews in the 1920s, plus a commentary volume by the editor.

Some workers in the *Slave Narratives* project photographed a limited number of the individuals they interviewed. An interested reader may view these pictures on microfilm or microfiche, usually in a research or specialized library. The facsimile editions do not contain them, however. Benjamin A. Botkin, who became folklore editor on the Writers' Project after it ended, included a few of the narrators' photographs in his volume, *Lay My Burden Down* (see below).

Botkin, B. A., editor. *Lay My Burden Down. A Folk History of Slavery.* Chicago: University of Chicago Press, 1945.

Furnas, J. C. *Goodbye to Uncle Tom.* New York: William Sloane Associates, 1956.

Gara, Larry. *Liberty Line: The Legend of the Underground Railroad.* Lexington: University of Kentucky Press, 1961.

Kemble, Frances Anne. *Journal of a Residence on a Georgian Plantation in 1838–1839.* New York: Harper & Brothers, 1863.

King, Wilma. *Stolen Childhood: Slave Youth in Nineteenth-Century America.* Bloomington and Indianapolis: Indiana University Press, 1995.

Lester, Julius. *To Be a Slave.* New York: Dial, 1968.

Olmsted, Frederick Law. *A Journey in the Seaboard Slave States.* New York: Dix & Edwards, 1856.

Rice, C. Duncan. *The Rise and Fall of Black Slavery.* New York: Harper & Row, 1975.

Rose, Willie Lee. *A Documentary History of Slavery in North America.* New York: Oxford University Press, 1976.

Scott, John Anthony. *Hard Trials on My Way.* New York: Alfred A. Knopf, 1974.

Stampp, Kenneth. *The Peculiar Institution: Slavery in the Ante-Bellum South.* New York: Alfred A. Knopf, 1956.

Sterling, Dorothy. *The Trouble They Seen.* New York: Doubleday, 1976.

Williamson, Joel. *After Slavery.* Chapel Hill (N.C.): University of North Carolina Press, 1965.

Yetman, Norman R. *Voices from Slavery.* New York: Holt, Rinehart and Winston, 1970.